Illana

P a t   J a c o b s

Why do it? Tom thought. What pushed sensible mature people to leave a comfortable life and spend thousands of dollars of their life savings to take risks in the middle of nowhere ...

Broome ... Fitzroy Crossing ... Darwin ... The Centre ...

It is the mid-nineties and Tom and Zoe Drewe, like thousands of others, are 'going around Australia'. Their journey, begun in certainty and on their terms, takes on its own momentum and compulsions, until they are driven as much as driving, and increasingly acted upon by the power and histories of the land whose surface they cross.

As with any journey there are risks of exposure: of unsought insights, startling new perspectives. In 'going inland' Tom and Zoe are confronted by the emptiness and silence of the interior — and the silences protecting the surfaces of their long marriage. Unexpectedly, they are navigating in unknown terrain. Finally — and unavoidably — they must face the question of their place in their own country; the long-reaching effects of their ancestors' migratory beginnings and of reconciling who they are with what they have discovered.

Compelling, moving, disturbing, this important and timely novel confronts the dark side of the Australian psyche, exploring what it means to be an Australian, and the nature of belonging.

Pat Jacobs was born in Collie, Western Australia. An historian, fiction writer and reviewer, she has received awards for both history and short fiction published in Australian journals and anthologies. Her first book, *Mister Neville*, a biography of A O Neville, was published by Fremantle Arts Centre Press in 1990 and short-listed for the Western Australian Premier's Award in 1991.

Phtotograph by Peter Payne.

Pat Jacobs

going In*land*

FREMANTLE ARTS CENTRE PRESS

First published 1998 by
FREMANTLE ARTS CENTRE PRESS
PO Box 158, North Fremantle
Western Australia 6159.
http://www.facp.iinet.net.au

Reprinted 2000.

Consulting Editor Wendy Jenkins.
Designer Marion Duke.
Production Coordinator Cate Sutherland.

Typeset by Fremantle Arts Centre Press
and printed by Sands Print Group, Western Australia.

National Library of Australia
Cataloguing-in-publication data

Jacobs, Pat, 1936—.
Going inland.

ISBN 1 86368 206 6.

I. Title.

A823.3

The State of Western Australia has made an investment in this project
through ArtsWA in association with the Lotteries Commission.

Publication of this title was assisted by the Commonwealth Government through
the Australia Council, its arts funding and advisory body.

For
Stephen, Ann and Mark

Acknowledgements

My thanks to Helen Fenbury and Julie Lewis for their patience and generosity in discussion and reading of the manuscript. Also to John Stanton for his valuable advice on Aboriginal desert art and related issues.

Geoffrey Bardon's essay on the Papunya Tula artists appeared in the catalogue for the National Gallery of Victoria exhibition *Mythscapes: Aboriginal Art of the Desert*. To my knowledge, there has been no retrospective exhibition of Papunya Tula artists at Araluen, Alice Springs, in recent years. I am indebted to Geoffrey Bardon for his permission to quote from the essay.

Adelaide Springs Historic Hotel is a fiction.

My thanks to HarperCollins for permission to quote from James McAuley's 'Captain Quiros' and 'Envoi' from the Collected Works, Imprint Edition, 1994.

Every effort has been made to obtain permission for the quotation from *An Duanaire 1600–1900; Poems of the Dispossessed* reproduced on page 196. Acknowledgement will appear in any subsequent edition. 'The County of Mayo', translated by George Fox from the Irish of Thomas Lavalle, was taken from a collection of Irish verse, edited by W B Yeats, published by Methuen in 1895.

I gratefully acknowledge the assistance of the Australia Council for the Arts in providing a project grant to complete the research for this book.

This is a fiction. Where actual people are named it is as public figures in a time.

Contents

Land of the inmost heart, searching for
which Men roam the earth ...

James McAuley
'Captain Quiros'

Going North

B r o o m e

The orchardist and his wife left their south-west valley in the grip of a cold winter. The fruit trees stretching bare branches up the slopes, the ground rimed with frost; the cold habit they had worn all their lives.

It was their first trip. They joined the exodus north, the long procession of caravans and campers, of gleaming LandCruisers, the tight-packed trailers with dinghies strapped on top, spreading up the coastal highway; part of the ritual urge that took hold in middle life — to go around Australia.

When the time came the departure was a release from ordinary life. Houses had been closed up or rented out. Affairs had been put in order. Families had been farewelled. It was an undertaking of months, circumnavigating the continent. As the travellers crossed the vast spaces, sometimes a sense of futility at their skimming passage across the surface would make them uneasy. They thought of it as home sickness.

11

In the years after the catharsis of the first journey north, retired couples would slow down and shorten the distance between stops. They would stay longer. Clustering together in groups in distant places. Resting. Putting their folding chairs out in the sun they would talk. Their conversations brief fugues; one taking up the theme before the other finished. They repeated themselves, their amnesia a rise and fall of flight from reality: the finality of packing up; the return journey which sapped their energy.

Tom and Zoe Drewe were in a hurry; they had to be back in a few months to harvest their fruit. The decision to go on the trip had been made in a hurry when Tom bought a second-hand campervan. It fitted neatly on the back of the farm's four-wheel drive truck. The economy meant they could go without delay.

Each morning they rose while it was still dark. In the penetrating desert chill, the woman made toast and coffee, filled a thermos while the man checked the truck and started the motor. The road unwound like a spool and they were avid for it. As the landscape changed and they entered unknown country, they became lighter. A weight, which was connected to their life at home, began to shift. They were boisterous, unsure of themselves without boundaries, as if habit had first to be unlearned in the body.

Their perceptions were affected by limitless horizons. They unfolded their map. They measured distance. They looked for landmarks. They read the signs. The idea of nothing as a measure of time passing, of sameness as the measure of change, surprised them.

The north-western coastal town straggled around a bay of brilliant azure water. Iron roofs and cyclone shutters showed blind faces to the street. Softened by a profusion of alien bougainvillea and coconut palms, the old houses drowsed through hot afternoons, unaffected by the new holiday resorts where white bodies sprawled around swimming pools seeking a winter tan. Like a 1920s postcard, conservative Australians took on the pose of Europeans in the tropics. Ice melting in tumblers, palm trees rustling, they practised a self-conscious hedonism.

A few kilometres out of town a trickle of more practised hedonists, with a long history, had found the fabled beach. There they dined à la carte in exotic architecture, surrounded by priceless Asian art works. The charming sleaze of a forgotten colonial outpost had been transformed into an oriental Folly; a last fling of Empire in the Antipodes.

Dazed with unaccustomed heat, visitors wandered in and out of shops in Chinatown. The women tried on pearl rings and pendants, pretending they might buy. The men endured it, taken with the novelty of the travelling life, the leisure which required that the hours be filled. Few knew or cared that Chinatown was not itself, but something else; the textures of the old and the new in a seamless hologram, ending at a corner or a laneway. The sudden view of a littered foreshore or the bare red plains baking in the sun revealed the thinness of the facade. The old town, created out of the violence and passion of the greed for pearls; the polyglot world of Aboriginal, Filipino, Japanese, Chinese and European was a chimera in continuous replay of its past.

In the Japanese cemetery, visitors walked the pathways between the austere headstones. Elegant brushstrokes held the enigma of who was buried there: pearldivers, caught in the *rapture of the deep*, where the colour fades to the same black and grey tones as the headstones. The women? Marooned forever? The sedate doll-figures in their glowing

kimonos waiting for their customers; their contracts —
promising they would be returned home — hidden with
their savings in a sandalwood box. Their etched faces fading
into other shapes, other bloodlines; leaving behind a nuance
in the single fold of an eyelid.

At the supermarket, Tom and Zoe replenished their
foodstock. They checked the quality of the fruit — last
season's apples from cold storage. They bought a newspaper
and waited for a free table at the cafe to drink coffee and
write postcards to their family like the other couples ...
drinking coffee ... writing postcards. They took the reflective
eddy of likeness surrounding them as a measure of their
own well-being. Unaccustomed to difference, they saw
themselves in others.

In the car park the Toyotas were lined up, caked with dust
and mud. The Aboriginal women loaded them with supplies
and children and drove off. Slipping through the gears with
flair. Gunning powerful motors past the museum holding
relics of their families' history.

*Before us here we have a display of chains which played
their part in the development of the State ... although it
may appear to border on medieval cruelty ... it was
necessary as journeys were long, running into weeks,
sometimes months. Accused and witnesses alike were
chained together in transport, fastened by the neck ...*

Fastened by the neck ... He read the caption a second time.
Only sixty years ago.

The orchardist was a practical man. He realised that,
given the ground temperatures in this country and the slow
passage of men on foot, the iron chains would heat up and
sear through the skin to the raw flesh beneath. He turned
away, to his wife, but she was looking at something else.

Only the coast, the lunatic fringe, remained the same. A

mesmeric force pulls the sea back to the horizon, baring the soft grey mud of the seabed, the underbelly, leaving the mangroves, deceptively benign, glistening in the sun. The tides move the ocean with a frightful power, indifferent to the brief meridian of the tourist season.

Near Streeter's jetty, where the *Last Pearling Lugger* was lashed tight against the tides, two men sat talking unnoticed by the tourists. The old man was a gifted artist. They were discussing a painting, a dream ceremony, concerning the rai spirits. 'What do they look like?' the anthropologist asked. 'They are small,' the old man answered, 'but they are just like us. They are all around us. There is one behind you right now.' The two men rested in the narrow patch of shade thrown by the jetty timbers, surrounded by the rai spirits visible to the old man. He was close to death and the boundaries between worlds were indistinct. His spiritual clarity was strong. He smiled with amusement and affection at the anthropologist.

The two couples met over drinks in one of the new cafes in Chinatown: spiders — cream soda and ice-cream — in a tall fluted glass. (A whim, surfacing after visiting the Sun open air theatre.) The rows of sagging deckchairs, the posters of Veronica Lake, Jon Hall and Sabu, smiling at them from the walls. Nostalgia freed them to exchange names and locations. They lived in nearby towns in the south-west. The orchardist and the chemist shared their attachment to the bland adventures of Saturday matinees and sighed for their innocence. The women smiled with indulgence.

Together, the two couples made plans to drive out along the thin arm of the peninsula to see a church built by Aborigines and missionary monks in the early years of the century. Travelling in company, they were confident about the expedition. To go into a community of Aboriginal people carried with it the aura of the adventurous. A childhood carryover of the forbidden, although none of this surfaced in their conversation. In the places they lived there was no language to express what they felt.

It was a rough, unsealed road, testing the skill of the men on the deep drifts of dry sand. It was far enough to disconnect them from the town. At the community office, not sure of the protocol, they were overly polite. 'We've come to see the church,' the chemist said, anxious to do the right thing. A man and woman leaning on the counter, engrossed in a conversation, gave them conflicting directions, laughing at the confusion. 'We'll show you,' they offered. 'No, no, thank you.' The visitors were definite. Awkward in their intrusion. They drove in the general direction indicated, past cottages, scattering playing children. Women hanging out their washing stopped to watch them pass. The road narrowed to a laneway, ending at a large shade tree where a group of people sat playing cards. The visitors reversed their vehicles, waving a greeting as they passed. They followed whichever track seemed most likely, passing the card-players a second time. Not looking. Grim with an embarrassed urgency to find the way.

The church floated incongruously on a sea of yellowed grass. White and solemn. Its bell tower pointing into a brilliant blue arc of sky. It looked Romanesque. Graceful yet sturdy. A European church belonging in the tight sculpted order of a European landscape. It was a link, however remote, with the familiar. They parked both vehicles under a shade tree and went in.

The altar gleamed in the soft opalescent reflection of pearl shell. Hundreds, even thousands of clam shells had been gathered to ornament its surface; the tabernacle, and the floor patterned in an inlaid mosaic. Everywhere the eye fell, a design glowed in the nacreous underwater light of the shells. Aboriginal motifs entwined with ancient Christian symbols in a cool studied beauty.

An old monk in a dusty brown cassock came slowly, crossing through the pews to the porch. He carried an oversize magnifying glass and a large alarm clock. The visitors raised eyebrows and smiled. 'It's a tea party. Alice will show up next,' Zoe whispered. The old monk bent his body to sit on a bench. He studied the clock through the magnifying glass.

'*Es ist Zeit*?' he whispered to his companions. They swayed around him, nebulous and dear. They were his eyes and ears, his speech. Since he could no longer hear it didn't matter what form the words took. He knew himself to be almost as amorphous as his companions. Sometimes it was the Spanish of the Benedictines, or the Nyul Nyul of the people. Sometimes the French or German the Trappists had used. He had heard them all. The little flames, the tongues of fire. The Holy Spirit made it all one. All one.

He studied the alarm clock through his magnifying glass, waiting. At noon they rose with him, his cloud of angels. They tolled the Angelus. The bell-rope vibrated in his hands, but he heard, clearly, in his head, the conch shell from the old days, calling the people. He swayed with the rhythm of the bell-rope, dizzy with it, his legs bending as if for purchase on a heaving deck. He had sailed the schooner up the coast with Bishop Torres, looking for a good place. The little Spaniard's *Tierra del Espíritu Santo*. Leaning over the side, the Bishop had called to him:

' ... *the sea is so like a polished mirror, it almost frightens one to look down ... the clouds reflected on the surface ... one feels dizzy with such illusory depths ...* '

The old monk clung to the bell-rope, remembering, closing his eyes against the milky swirl of light. That had been before the war, the first one. Before the church was built. Bishop Raible had danced with the men, the cockatoo feathers in his hair as white as his skin in the moonlight. The men came for their sons in the night to finish their law business. In the morning, the dormitory would be empty.

So many, so many had come to work this field of souls and gone away. He had stayed. He could not remember why. It didn't matter now.

Hungry and thirsty, the visitors unpacked their chairs and table and set up their picnic in the shade. The women sliced tomatoes and cucumbers and chicken, opened cake tins and set out plates and paper serviettes. The men poured cool drinks, and they all sat, watching children playing on the field. Somewhere a generator started up. It was a regular peaceful sound, a reminder of the slow routine of farm-life, of self-containment.

They could see the tops of coconut palms across the field. 'It must be the spring and the lagoon,' Zoe said. 'And the coast is there somewhere.'

'We could be in the Caribbean, in Jamaica or somewhere like that. On a plantation. It is so quiet,' the chemist's wife agreed. 'There should be more places like this.' They passed each other the salad and chicken, polite in their new friendship.

A woman was walking quickly across the field, swerving to avoid the playing children. They sat in their folding chairs, too lazy for conversation, watching her figure become more distinct. They could see that she was young. She held her head down, walking quickly, in a fluid, half-running gait.

They were startled when they realised her purpose. The women stood up and began packing away the remains of the meal. The men moved in their chairs, flexing their legs; a reflex of preparedness.

She was puffing slightly when she reached them. There was an elusive elegance in her speech, the faintest lisp. An urgency.

'Are you going to Broome?' She held them with her eyes.

The men were wary. 'Ah, no,' one said.

'You are going to Lombadina?'

'Where's that?'

'It's the next place, down the road.'

'We haven't decided yet.'

'Can you give me a lift to the crossroad then?' Her skin was dark, but its colour did not hide the bruised, split skin over her cheekbone.

'There's nowhere for you to sit. See? There's only two seats.'

She had already seen ...'I could fit in the back.'

They shook their heads.

'Please,' she said, looking behind her, scanning the field. 'Only to the crossroad. I'll walk then ... '

The men folded the chairs and table, looking away. They packed the gear in the trucks. The wives waited, motionless, leaving it to the men. Abruptly the woman turned away. She didn't hurry as she had before. She walked slowly, her head down.

They drove carefully on the way out of the community, the two vehicles close together. A burst of music came from the office as they passed; a vibrant rich harmony. The satellite dish on the roof glinted in the sun.

They didn't stop until they were past the crossroad, until

they had turned onto the road back to town. They rummaged in the remnants of the picnic and found drinks and biscuits. They moved around to stretch their legs as they ate and drank.

'Godforsaken bloody country,' one of the men said. 'Just scrub — nothing in it.'

'They run cattle here by the look of it.'

'They want to do something about this road.'

The women spoke quietly together. 'Maybe we should have ... You know ... she was frightened.'

'You can't get involved ...' They agreed, but the charm of the girl's accent, her soft voice, lingered.

They packed away the biscuits and drink containers, keeping everything neat and tidy.

'Let's go,' the men said. 'We don't want to be stuck out here in the dark.' They were slightly uncomfortable with each other. No one suggested they meet again.

One vehicle pulled out and, when the dust settled, the other followed.

The Crossing

The road arrowed across the plain, skirting a mountain range, at times cutting through banks of tilted strata. The dark red seams, stripped of overburden, revealed their history to anyone who could read stone. Slender white-trunked trees grew directly out of the rock like compressed *essence*.

The absence of a recognisable topsoil made Tom and Zoe Drewe conscious that they were in a different country. They came from the sunklands of river and valley where the deep loam offered no resistance; where the habits of life were a soft, unimpeded erosion of time. Now the familiar was reduced to the interior of the vehicle: their bodies, their possessions and certainties packed inside it. They waved to passing vehicles, reaching out. Left only with each other when the road was clear.

There was nothing to indicate that the land had been used. No signs of settlement. Except one, hand-lettered, with an arrow pointing: *Noonkanbah.*

'Remember Noonkanbah?' Tom said.

'Vaguely.' She remembered it though, remembered the year: 1980, the long convoy of trucks loaded with drilling equipment heading north with a police escort, confronting them each night on television news. The strong planes of the black faces, the soft hesitant voices of the old men trying to explain — the emotion ... Each night, the tension ... the unimaginable possibility of the familiar order of life splitting apart. It had been like the beginning of a war ... she remembered that. Their neighbour, Gerry Falcon, had come over to talk to Tom about joining the convoy, hiring his truck out, telling him there was good money in it, a bit of excitement. No one ever mentioned it now. It was as though it had never happened.

Closer to the settlement they could see the evidence of past destruction. Litter was wedged in the crowns of rivergums. Broken tree limbs were piled against boulders, like bones whitening in the sun. They were on a vast floodplain. The elevated road was a safe flood crossing but its height above the ground challenged their knowledge of the possibilities of water, of rain and river as they knew it. Who could ever be sure. Once a vehicle started on the crossing there was no turning back.

They parked in the street. Between the scatter of buildings there was a patch of grass with shade trees. Groups of people sat and lolled on the ground. In the afternoon heat and glare their blackness merged with the shadows of the trees; a contrast of still yellow light and dark rippling movement. Children and dogs rolled and played. Voices were raised then subdued. With the windows down, Tom and Zoe watched, soporific with the heat, listening to the strange gutturals, the rapid explosions of a language they didn't know.

In the tourist office in Derby they had read that a linguistic centre for the reclamation and recording of languages was located here at the Crossing; a pool of knowledge being refilled from the fragments of tribal languages. Each different; with connected meanings, but different. Not just one. Momentarily, Tom and Zoe were unwilling to leave the truck. They were not in a foreign country. They were in their own country — and yet ... Those who owned the language were a closed circle. Travellers like themselves could move only on the perimeter, unaware that the sounds they uttered were peripheral to the continuum of meaning between the people and the landscape they were passing through. Embedded in the language the Drewes spoke were the foreign shapes of a different hemisphere.

'How far is it to the next place?' Tom asked.

Zoe refolded the map. 'It's too far. We'll be driving in the dark.'

Tom eased his shoulders, hunching over the steering wheel. 'We'll stay here. I don't think I want to compete with the road trains.'

It was a hazard. The trucks roared out of the night. Lights blazing. Juggernauts. Forcing travellers off the road.

They left the campervan parked on the verge and walked down the street. The young men let them pass, ignored them as though they were invisible They were jostled, though, by old men who appeared to be drunk. Or was it near blindness? Their eyes were clouded and milky, unseeing and uncaring of whom they stumbled against. They were so thin, the old men. Their shirt and pants seemed to cover merely bones. In the supermarket, mothers filled trolleys while children played on the turnstile and chased each other down the aisles. Zoe smiled at the children, wanting recognition, and they smiled back, their big eyes cheeky and friendly. On the way back to the truck she followed Tom, letting him find a path through the people, keeping her eyes down, embarrassed at her own nervousness.

The caravan park confronted them with its ugliness, the rutted track between bays indicating that it had been a quagmire in the Wet Season. A row of concrete slabs, each with a rusted steel pole carrying an electricity outlet, waited for the unwary who had misjudged their journey and landed here.

'We'll leave early. Don't unpack anything,' Tom said. Tiredness made them tense, clumsy with the few movements they had to make to settle themselves for the night. In silence they skirted each other. One wrong word could release a flood. This was not the place. What seemed an almost deliberate lack of convenience sharpened their irritation to a razor edge. Zoe used the broom handle to knock a cluster of drink cans and a cracked plastic bucket away from the tap.

'Leave it,' he said. 'Don't do anything.'

Tom had gone to have a look around. Zoe lay on the bunk, the fan blowing directly on to her bare skin. It was so easy to make mistakes. They had been careless in Derby. It had been Sunday. Everything closed. There had been no queue of caravans at the service station. No one to ask. The wide streets had been almost empty of people and cars and, out of boredom, they had decided to go on. They had refuelled, bought milk and a loaf of frozen bread and left, glad to be moving again. The map gave you the names and the distance but it didn't tell you anything else.

She wiped her face and arms with the damp cloth, closing

her eyes with pleasure at the brief, delicious chill of evaporation. Disjointed images of the repulsive grey mud exposed on the tidal flats at Derby, the broken glass and aluminium cans scattered in the street, were in her mind. She wanted to complain about the heat, and the griminess that was creeping into their clothes, filtering into the van. *It is not my fault*, she wanted to shout at him. *This is not where we should be. This is not the place.* The ugliness, the strangeness. It was all wrong. And Tom — Tom was not sympathetic. She had caught a hint, some emanation coming from him that he was aware of her discomfort and unmoved by it. As though an antagonism had come into existence between them.

She woke to find Tom offering her a cup of tea. 'You should have put the catch on the door,' he told her. 'You don't want to lay around like that.'

'I didn't intend to go to sleep.' She drew the sheet around her. 'Did you find anything interesting?'

'Yes. There's a hotel down the road. We can have dinner there. Oh — you'd better get a bit dressed up. It looks pretty flash.'

They grinned at each other. It was a countryman's phrase; a farmer's disdain of unnecessary opulence. It reconnected them, with home and each other.

The showers were empty; basic but clean. The water was plentiful and hot. She let it pour over her, shampooing her hair twice to get rid of the dust. Despite the shelter of a hat and suncream her skin looked lightly tanned, but this was deceptive. The colour, she knew, was a pin-pricking of tiny freckles. Her skin would not take the sun, her red hair the sign of incompatibility. She studied herself in the steamy mirror, wishing as always that it was otherwise. Wishing for the grainy olive skin Tom had inherited from somewhere, or even the dense white skin of her mother; not this odd response of pigment, her body's failure to overcome the memory of a cold place.

She applied make-up. A bit of colour. A touch of lipstick and eyeshadow, blending beige foundation with the freckles in a skilful cover-up. Slipping on the loose top and skirt which had been rolled up for weeks, she thought of a long cold gin and tonic, with ice and lemon, and something elaborate to eat. Finally she sprayed a mist of perfume over her arms and neck, calling up a faint childhood evocation of incense, of anointing — the thurible swinging — *the body is the temple of the soul*. She was ready.

Outside, women had emerged from the battered vans which seemed to be permanent homes. A few children ran around and men had appeared, their mud-stained vehicles parked alongside the vans. They must work somewhere. Mining ... or road building. The place seemed to be a work camp, with no pretense of being anything else. The men came to earn money and the women came to claim whatever their men had left to give. Who could live here? Zoe wondered, thinking of the women, day after day. Waiting in the caravans for the men to come home. Numbing themselves with sleep through the hot afternoons. The children enclosed with the flickering television or video screens. Every van had an antenna and a rusting airconditioner on its roof. She thought of her own sprawling white house on the side of the valley, the orchard surrounding it. She loved the symmetry of the lines of trees laden with fruit. And the rounded green hills, seeping water; it seemed abundant and unbearably sweet in comparison to this barren place. She missed the intricate cycles of her life, the seasons and rituals which shaped them. She could never be the same person here. It would change her. Already, in the time they'd been travelling, she had noticed small changes. She had lost weight. The lightness gave her an energy, a momentum. A kind of impatience to keep moving, to get to wherever they were going. The energy had sharpened her, fed the edge of irritation and impatience between her and Tom. It appeared and disappeared like a dark rim on the horizon, an unexplored place in their life.

In the supermarket, amongst the women, their large dark soft bodies, she had felt a flicker of awareness pass between them and her; a swift dart of affinity. It was the children, their children, her interest in them — but they had warded her off. She had felt it and it had made her want to insist that they acknowledge her. She felt excluded from something female ... She was used to the sodality of women: sisters, daughter, friends. The rejection had disconcerted her.

She draped their damp towels over the table, unwilling to make even the minor gesture of hanging them outside to dry. Tom locked the van and they walked together down the road to the office. She waited outside while Tom went in to book them in for the night. A short distance away a group of men stood talking. In the strong glare of the late afternoon sun, one of them seemed to glisten and glint in a haze of white. She narrowed her eyes against the glare as she walked towards them. He was a young man, a boy, dressed in white moleskins stretched tight on his legs, narrow over his polished riding boots. His white shirt danced with points of light, the white broad-brimmed hat was pushed back from his face and his skin glowed with a soft light; the golden down on his cheeks and bare arms enclosed him in an aureole. His unlikely beauty captivated Zoe. She looked

27

at him as much as she could without drawing his attention. The men he was with were affected by his beauty too. She could see the way they hung on his words, leaning in towards him, laughing when he laughed. He took them out of themselves: the heat, the dirt, their jaded women and fretful children waiting for them. Where he was, where he came from, was where they wanted to be. Youth, strength. He was life as they had dreamed it ... He was the promise of it.

Tom joined her and they walked past the group of men. The light — the moment of vision — had gone. 'Did you see that boy? Dressed up.'

'From one of the cattlestations probably, in town for a night out.'

They crossed the road and walked down a path lined with lush gardens. A tall metal fence tipped with ornamental spears enclosed the buildings. Imported palms planted in close groves rose above it, completing the concealment of the interior. He inserted a disc into the gate lock to open it.

'I had to register so we could get in — security,' he said.

Inside the compound, the path led to a swimming pool and a bar. A white-coated attendant showed them to a table overlooking the pool. Small groups of people sat around talking and drinking. 'A coach came in this afternoon,' the attendant said, 'Germans mainly, some French and Italian. It's Hawaiian night tonight, or the à la carte.' The tables filled, more were brought out. Taped music was turned on. Noise eddied around them. Voices. Other languages.

A couple took the vacant chairs at their table. 'Do you mind?' the woman asked, smiling. Zoe, pleased at the chance of company, smiled back, welcoming them. 'Are you from around here?' the woman asked, her American drawl identifying her. Zoe hesitated. She was *not from here*, but to say she was from the south, she would have to explain. The south was different ... Tom spoke first. 'We're Australian — from down south.'

'Did you hear that Norman.' She tugged at her husband. 'These folks are from "down south." Are you "going around" too? There are so many of you in your trailers. Is it the season for it?' She leaned over the table. 'It's crowded tonight. The Europeans don't mix,' she said to Tom in an exaggerated whisper. 'They've come from Kununurra today — that huge lake. They stay one night and go on to the river gorges tomorrow. Windjana, where your famous Aboriginal resistance fighter was killed.' Politely she pressed the point. 'Have you done the boat trip up the gorge?'

'We've just arrived,' Tom said.

'We're from Boston. I'm Elsa and this is Norman. Every year he drags me off somewhere. Last year it was New Zealand.'

Courtesy required that they introduce themselves. 'We have a property in the country,' Zoe said. 'Tom is a fruit-grower.'

'Oh, do you both work at the fruit growing?'

'Zoe is a painter,' Tom said abruptly.

'Oh. Then you must be interested in the work the women are doing here. They're marvellous artists.' She regarded them with shrewd eyes. 'Walmadjeri and Wonggadjungga? We've bought several.'

To cover her ignorance of the local artists Zoe talked to Elsa about the south, the valley and the farm, making it even more beautiful than it was. Describing it as she had left it in winter: the mist clinging to the river at the foot of the green hills; hearing her own voice, unable to stop. How both their families had always lived there. Elaborating a myth of settlement that she had not known existed, complete in her mind, until now.

Enclosed by the glamour of palm trees in the warm tropical night and the easy comfort of the Americans, her spirit expanded and rose. Charmed by her own myth, she felt secure and benevolent. She tossed her red-gold hair, knowing it would catch the light, seeing in the woman's concentration on her a reflection of the intrinsic value of her story. The woman encouraged her, fixing her large eyes on Zoe, excluding the men who talked quietly to each other. They lingered over coffee as Zoe tried to explain to Elsa her friendly overture to the women in the supermarket and how they had rebuffed her, how she had been afraid walking through the crowd in the street. Elsa nodded and smiled as Zoe tried to describe the phenomenon of the boy in the sunlight, the illusion of the aureole of light and how the men surrounding him had seemed captivated.

Tom stood abruptly. Easing himself from behind the table. 'It's late,' he said to Zoe. 'We've got an early start in the morning.'

The gate swung shut behind them, closing off the lights and music, the noise and laughter within the compound. Outside was a sea of darkness. There were no familiar landmarks to orient by. Their night vision failed them. Nothing known or certain materialised. Zoe felt over-stimulated, taken out of herself. 'Where are we? Where are we going?' She clung to Tom, stumbling on the rough ground. He trod carefully, leading slightly. 'The road is here somewhere. If I can find it we'll walk down the middle. It's only around the bend.' Bush brushed against them. There was no moon, only the intense blaze of the stars if they looked up. There was a rustle of something light getting out of their way. 'I hope we don't step on a snake,' Tom muttered. 'I can't see a bloody thing.'

Zoe moaned. 'I want to go back to the hotel.'

'We can't. I haven't got the key anyway. I had to hand it in.' Behind them the hotel was lost, its lights and noise, the familiar machinery which drove it receding, like an elegant cruise ship, leaving them marooned. Ahead of them, somewhere, there was a sudden outburst of angry shouts and screams, the breaking of glass. They stopped. Waited. Glad of the dark now. Listening to the sound of a car taking off at speed, tyres skidding on gravel. 'Come on,' Tom said, 'we have to keep going.' They moved quietly, relieved to reach the wide intersection of roads. They crossed to the caravan park.

The battered steel mesh gates were closed — padlocked with a circle of chain. Tom shook them in frustration. The ugliness, the apathy and indifference which hung over the place looked commonplace and familiar. 'We *can't* be locked out,' Zoe said. 'We have to get in.'

'We'll have to climb over.'

Tom went first, depressing the strands of barbed wire at the top, hauling Zoe upwards. Despite his help, Zoe was awkward — half laughing.

'*Come on,*' he said, 'I can think of things I'd rather do than get a drunk woman over a six-foot gate.'

'Like what?' She teased him. The barbed wire bit into her thigh, tearing the flimsy cloth of her skirt. Startled, she cried out and overbalanced.

Down, down she fell, like a star falling out of the dark night. Her pale softness smothering him, winding him, robbing him of speech. There was no getting away. He was offbalance, out of place. He could have wept at the keenness of his disappointment. Nothing was as he thought it would be. He felt foolish and diminished and

31

worse than that — betrayed. Tricked into a shamefulness that did not belong to him. He could not put into words what they had lost — or given away — both of them — but it had left a bitter taste..

They struggled to their feet, like clumsy dancers locked in an embrace.

In the van they circumnavigated each other, hampered by the narrow space. 'It's all right,' she said, 'it's nothing,' shedding the ripped skirt. 'See? It's nothing.' Her voice rippled over him, filling the small space with her murmuring. Soothing. Restoring them both by habit. 'It's all right,' she said. 'It'll be all right.'

They made tea and tended Zoe's wound, a long ragged tear oozing blood. 'They weren't tourists, you know,' Tom said, 'the Americans. They've been working here. He's a historian and she's a linguist. They poke around, talking to people. Recording. Digging up old stuff. He told me a story he'd heard ... after a really bad flood someone found the carcass of a steer — in the debris. There were all these extra bones ... The steer had been gutted and a man's body stuffed inside. He was telling me about the killings — massacres, he called them — around this area in the 1890s. He asked me if I knew anything about Aboriginal resistance in the south.'

'What did you say?'

'I told him ... about Pinjarra. It's all I could remember. I felt so bloody ignorant ... Wanted to know if I employed black labour ... '

They were silent.

In his mind, Tom saw a man standing over a body, a shotgun against the temple, shattering the bone. The body convulsing. He had shot a horse that way once. Quickly. Coldly. But unable to quell the rush of adrenalin. Why put the body in the steer's carcass? To conceal the murder? The dead weight levered into the river? Could a man do that alone? Or had it been a warning not to kill cattle — left rotting in the heat.

'The cowboy,' Zoe said, 'the beautiful cowboy. It must have been the brass studs on his shirt, catching the sun ... He looked like an angel. A visitation. I wish I hadn't told Elsa that.'

'You talk too much,' he said to her.

They lay in the dark, listening: the angry shouting, a woman screaming, the sound of a car stopping. Headlights illuminating the night. They whispered to each other, as if afraid of discovery. Unsure of their status in a strange country. It was safer to stay out of sight.

'As soon as the gates are open we'll leave. We've got enough fuel.'

'It will be early,' Zoe said. 'The men start work early.'

'We'll have breakfast later, on the road.'

Sleepless, they waited for the first light.

Landfall

The college was closed. They drove around the perimeter of the complex, peering down the deserted walkways. The tourist guidebook hadn't mentioned the Batchelor Aboriginal College. Sprinklers swung arcs of water across the lawns. It was the only sound.

Feeling exposed as trespassers, they parked and walked a little way into the gardens. It was the mid-semester vacation, but there was a sense that at any moment doors would swing open, people with a purpose would emerge, carrying bags and books, voices would call and talk and laugh; activity would suddenly begin. That the people would be black required a shift in perception. Tom and Zoe had never been on an Aboriginal campus. The distance between their experience of student days — the privileged college for the sons of rich farmers and university scholarships for clever country girls — made them uncomfortable.

'You'd think there would be something about this place in the travel guide,' Tom said. 'It's well-established.'

'There's nothing.' Zoe had the guide with her. 'I've checked. It makes you wonder what else we don't know about.'

They walked along a verandah, reading the signs on doors. *Education Studies, Community Studies ... Health ... Communication ...* Zoe paused to look through a window. Things had changed and they hadn't been aware of it.

In the morning they would make an early fast run into Darwin. They'd asked around and discovered that it was the thing to do. Caravan parks in Darwin were hard to get into. Good sites were at a premium. Despite their intention to resist the urge to get the best site, to miss nothing ... to get it right at any cost — they had got caught up in it. They made the excuse that they were going to stay longer and have a rest from travelling, that the tropical climate was tiring and they wanted the extra comfort. When they made a telephone call to a new popular caravan resort to reserve a site they were told that they would have to join the queue.

It would be a race. Tom cleaned the truck and fuelled it.

Restless, with the afternoon to fill in, Zoe read the brochures on Litchfield Park, studying the coloured photographs of the waterfalls in the kiosk: *Do the waterfall crawl* the caption read. *Bookings essential. Numerous cascades falling through dense monsoonal rainforest ...* They had argued in the end.

'It's only thirty kilometres away, on a good road. To come all this way — I thought that's why we were doing this; to see the country.'

'We can see it on the way back. I don't want to get the vehicle dirty.'

'On the way back you'll want to keep going.'

'Haven't you got some washing to do? Why don't you go for a walk — or just have a rest ...'

In the end, they had driven the short distance to a lake formed by excavation. The kiosk manager had said it was the local swimming hole. The track wound through hillocks of mining waste, bare of vegetation. The hard clay pan where they parked glittered with broken glass. The body of water was motionless and dark. Zoe, to whom water and swimming were familiar elements, was reluctant. She walked along the edge, unwilling to enter. 'It looks dead, I can't swim in that.'

'Plenty of others do,' Tom said, 'by the look of it.'

There were the ash beds of numerous fires, the grey crumpled remains of beer cans heaped around them.

Taking her sandals off Zoe stepped into the water. It circled her thighs in an oily chilling cold, lying heavy against her skin. She shuddered, losing her nerve, wading quickly back to the verge. 'Come and look,' she called, 'you can't see through the water.' A metre from the shore the water was dark brown and impenetrable. 'There's something wrong with it. It's awful,' she said. In the metallic light of a monsoonal afternoon the waste dumps and the still brown water were sinister.

'I thought you wanted to swim?'

'Not here.'

He started the truck and drove in silence. Zoe covered her face with her hands, as if to shut out the sight of the waste dumps. But it was his silence against which she had no certainty. The sudden presence of this cold region in their relationship undermined her. If they had gone to the water-falls, the pools shrouded in palms and ferns, the life there, the play of light on water and foliage would have kept them buoyant. One day, the shadow of their intimacy would take its real shape and confront them.

They left in the dawn cool, but others had already gone.

There was an excitement to it: Darwin, Cyclone Tracy, the reborn city, the northern edge of the continent. Tom was energised by the imperative of the race. Poised and focused. Nothing overlooked or fumbled. His mastery enveloped Zoe. It was seductive. She had no need to think or plan. In the long even plane of their life, their spheres of activity and convergence were clearly defined. She had forgotten, or never really known, this part of him; the focused energy, the competitive edge. Lulled by the warmth of the cab, the monotonous landscape, she drifted, trying to pinpoint the vague idea that he had a world of his own in which he was different; a world in which she, their children, the intricate sphere of family life was separate — and peripheral. It was possible (was it possible?) that he entered and left her world at will? That it did not contain the whole of him — as it did her. It had enclosed her and left him free. The silence — was a way out.

A shaft of memory opened: the aroma of cedar oil from the piano, sunlight through the verandah door hived with dust motes, catching the faded watercolour of Venice on the wall above the piano. Her father's voice merging with the glissando of arpeggios. The intolerable sweet melancholy, the ache in the bone; the racial echo of lament which bound them together. *The harp that once ... through Tara's Hall ...*

'What did you say?'

'Nothing,' she answered, 'an old song.' They had entered the outskirts of the city.

'Have you got the map?' Tom asked. 'We'll have to turn soon.' She smoothed it on her knee. She was good with maps.

Zoe sat at the only vacant shaded pool-side table, spreading out her things to discourage others from joining her.

Middle-aged men and women sat in the sun, their skin turning scarlet, sipping cans of cool drink and eating crisps. Their bodies were not comfortable with the humid heat. They endured it as long as they could, then lowered themselves into the pool, swimming a few strokes, floating.

Only the winners of the race that morning had the freedom of the facilities of the resort, and these were the rewards: the swimming pool, the games room. After shopping at the enormous airconditioned Plaza, the *Largest in the Southern Hemisphere*, they could laze by the pool, or go back to their *en suite ablution block* and shower in privacy. The unpainted concrete blocks with a shower, toilet and a washing trough, were the luxury they had competed for. The losers, who had mistimed their arrival, or not joined the queue, came to the pool fence and looked in. They tried the gates. Shook them in frustration at being locked out. They went back to their caravans lined up against the boundary fence, without power or water.

In the melee at the registration counter next morning there would be arguments when they found their overnight stay didn't count. By then the queue was tightly packed. No one was about to give up their place.

Zoe watched, through the shield of her sunglasses, as an elderly man, his wife beside him, argued with the pool attendant to be allowed to use the pool shower-room. The man was upset. He took his hat off and rubbed his forehead with the back of his hand. She saw then that he was old. His wife was anxious, worried that he would lose his temper. It's too much for them, she thought. The rules, the aggressiveness; the pace. It was not what they had expected. She moved her chair so she could see them walk back. Their van was an old Viscount, big and heavy. They had a Holden Statesman; green mesh was fitted across the radiator grille, a canvas waterbag hung from the roo bar. Fishing rods were tied along the roof. The old man had rigged a temporary awning with a piece of canvas, tying it to the fence. Like the others caught out, they had not unhitched. The travel-worn outfit stood out amongst the pop-top Coromals and Land Rovers, the Jayco Slimlines and Toyotas. With their roll-out awnings, wind deflectors and Reese tow hitches, the airconditioners and television aerials, built-in showers and toilets, the new outfits were sleek and correct.

There were tricks to it. Zoe had noted the library when they drove to the shopping plaza. Tom went looking for minor pieces of equipment and she went looking for information. She photocopied a page from the reference book. Uranium had been mined at Rum Jungle until 1963 and processing of the stockpiled ore continued until 1971. The plant and machinery had been dumped in the open-cut, the landscape left devastated and the river biologically dead for seventy-five kilometres ... Under the surface of the dark inert lake was a phantasmagoria of wrecked and twisted machinery. It was dead. Dead water in a dead landscape. She shuddered. The tourist information on Batchelor hadn't mentioned it. It would be easier not to, she could see that. On the way in to Darwin, travellers didn't stay long.

They shook out their good clothes and went to the Mindil Beach market to eat — and watch the sunset. The blood-red ball falling into a limpid tropical sea, where you couldn't swim because of sea wasps, the sharks and the odd salt water crocodile. Where the boat people came out of the north, drifting in on the tide, the overcrowded wooden boats low in the water; faces stretched tight with strain. Watching the coast. The Makassan came down 'like a wolf on the fold' ...

No. There were no wolves in Makassar. Tigers, maybe. Once. Dark traders, out of the unknown. Xenophobia. Headlines: THE NORTH HAS NO DEFENCE AGAINST INVASION. Darwin bombed (and the defenders fled to the south ... refugees jamming the road). Then the cyclone — on Christmas morning — blew it away. The horror! Like Sennacherib's ruined ransacked city. Who were the Assyrians anyway? Maps change and people and places are lost to history.

In the teeming market Zoe clung to Tom's arm. They stayed close together, moved and pushed by the dense crowd. In the background, the insistent half-tones of a gamelan orchestra set the tempo. Aromas of hot sesame oil, garam masala and garlic, of spicy curry, gusted over them. The refugees worked like demons over the roaring gas flames. Piles of mangos and pawpaws, great bunches of bananas, were pulverised into long cool drinks. In the sudden fall of night, faces glowed and streamed with the heat. Middle-aged hippies had come out of their hideaways and squatted over piles of cheap jewellery, high on ganja. Leaning against a tree, a man, his blackness merging into the night, sat with one leg outstretched, the sound of the didgeridoo matching the heartbeat; a deep and vibrant pulse of sound. Beside him his partner bargained with a black American tourist: fifteen hundred, twelve hundred, a thousand, black man's discount brother? Fuck you brother, laughing. Everywhere racks of tea-towels and T-shirts with Dreaming mantras: basic patterns for the tourist trade, or intricate limited edition with artwork copyright. Dreaming, dreaming. Over everything the Dreaming question, answer, meaning; gaudy on coffee cups, ashtrays, Raku pottery. Children, asleep, curled on soft piles of Taiwan merchandise. The scent of frangipani, strong and pure, hiding the dank smell of the mangrove flats. An alluring edge, hiding the secret inner aridity (Charles Darwin gliding past in the *Beagle* taking notes. *The answers were inside!*). A phantom island, a phobic landfall: paradise of the dispossessed.

At Kakadu, on the edge of the escarpment, at Ubirr, under the overhang, there was an answer. The ancient spidery lines, faded red against the stone, traced the beginning. Elongated figures danced the passage of the days, depicting, with elegant certainty, ancient beings in the act of living.

Below, the vast primordial wetland simmered and boiled with life. Savage and overpowering in its fecundity.

Tourists, faint and exhausted from their climb to the escarpment, came back clamouring for refreshing drinks; for nourishment of their own kind. Safely enclosed in the crocodile-shaped hotel, they chattered and laughed, bought souvenirs in a competitive fury, and missed the point — that they were subsumed in a totem of the Gagadju people.

Outside, in the terrible heat of the afternoon, the land sang to itself.

Tom and Zoe left Darwin in a hurry, their energy faltering under the onslaught of humidity. They could not engage with this city, the casino and hotels, the new showy buildings giving way suddenly to the half-built. The spreading suburbs. The raunchy rhythm of a hot tropical town re-creating itself with a febrile energy. They wanted the road again, the smooth clean momentum of escape.

Zoe said nothing when they passed the road to Litchfield and the cascades. (It would remain the lost opportunity. A *Shangri-la*, forever missed.) Now, like Tom, she was impatient to move on. It was not the kind of terrain where you lingered. They had taken on the mannerisms of transience, pulling into parking bays to eat a snack, exchanging greetings with others arriving or leaving, caught in the imperative of reaching a destination. Distance absorbed them, the horizon, the point on the map. There was nothing to hold them, nothing that claimed them.

The highway dissected the landscape like a magnetic strip, drawing the life of the region to its verge. The refuelling stops were small intense points of activity. Aboriginal groups sat or lolled under the sparse shade of trees, watching. At a one-bowser roadhouse, Tom kept the motor running while Zoe went in to buy some cans of cool drink. Two Filipina women slouched on the grubby counter, their eyes dull. Mail order brides, Zoe thought, as she took the cans and hurried out. What a place to be dumped — with no way out. At another, busier stop, road trains roared in with air-brakes hissing, their engines ticking with heat in the truck bays while the drivers ordered a meal in the restaurant. A white girl serving take-away food played a one-act virtuoso role with a crowd of black children. In the brief span of time available she controlled and dispensed their needs, calling them by name, berating, teasing. Sending some out, calling others back. They were her cast, her foil, and they played to her, each knowing their part. It was a performance for travellers played with energy and panache; a white/black dialectic in the outback. Tourists spilling out of a coach were engrossed. When the coach left, the children vanished and the girl rested, sullen and detached, between performances.

On a stretch of bare plain they stopped at a dusty weather-stained building, surrounded by a garrison of rusting fuel drums. It was a tavern as well as a fuel stop. An English girl, with heavy breasts barely contained in a singlet top, cornflower blue eyes and a south county accent, served them cold lemonade. Here the practice of boredom had been raised to an art form. The walls and ceilings were papered with money from other countries, bar coasters, travel stickers. Bottletops and matchstick folders were nailed to available surfaces. Aluminium tabs from cans, threaded on cord, hung in loops. There was an edge of obsession to it, the narrow focus of the collector creating meaning out of the accumulated trivia. The English girl was listless, caught in the torpor of a dead end, waiting for the energy to move on.

The fuel stops were the points where myths were transmitted. The man fuelling Tom's truck told him of the traveller 'who had a Villa Nova like yours on the back of a truck, lost his wife on this stretch of highway.' The traveller stopped to fuel up. His wife, who had been sleeping in the Villa Nova, got out to go to the toilet. When she came back the truck was gone. A traveller on a motor bike offered her a lift to chase her husband. Unaware that his wife was no longer in the slow-moving van, the husband had been amazed to see her hurtling past on the pillion of a motor bike, waving frantically, disappearing from view.

'Did he catch up with her?'

The fuel attendant shrugged. 'It's like those two young blokes a few years back. Took off from a station, trying to make it across to the Tanami. Only kids. Out there on their own. Didn't stand a chance. Hard way to go ... out there.'

'I read about a young bloke, from the east,' Tom said. 'It happened around here somewhere. He was looking for parts for his four-wheel drive. Couple of blokes took him out the bush, shot him, buried him in an antheap. Do you know anything about that?'

'They got them,' the man said, suddenly uninterested. 'Gun crazy some of these bastards.' He took Tom's money and moved on to the next vehicle.

They travelled in silence, subdued by images of the brutal unpredictability they might encounter. The red line on the strip map from Darwin to Port Augusta was crowded with names and captions. Map readers could mistake it for a zone of settled population and community. But it was deceptive. 'What happened?' Zoe said, only half-mocking. 'Where did everybody go?' Spreading out from the highway was a tracery of fine lines — tracks to gold, tin, wolfram and bismuth mines, cattle stations, creeks, springs. Memorials to dead explorers, to the building of the overland telegraph, to a hungry vision that had already peaked and faded, leaving only traces.

They passed Pine Creek without stopping, but the name prompted Zoe to rummage in her bag of maps and information. 'By 1888 there were three thousand Chinese navvies working on the Darwin to Pine Creek railway,' she read out. 'They weren't allowed to cross *an imaginary line one thousand miles south of Darwin* without paying a ten pound tax. What happened to them I wonder?'

'Some of them drifted south, following the railways, or the gold ...' Tom told her. 'There was an old Chinaman who had a garden down near the river in town.'

'In our town? Why would he have gone there?'

'They mined tin in the early days. There was a goldmine too. And then there was the main rail line from the city; that took years. My grandfather used to visit him — the Chinaman. They'd sit out the back of his shed and talk.' *He remembered ... going in the sulky, sitting up beside his grandfather. Being afraid to enter the dark, strange-smelling hut. Being*

given liquorice and told to wait in the vegetable garden. It was
something they did together, he and his grandfather, something
that was not mentioned at home ... the first secret. 'I can't
remember what they talked about, I was too young, but I
think it was goldmining.'

'In 1879, they outnumbered the Europeans in the Territory
by seven to one,' Zoe read out, 'the Europeans must have
been in a panic ...'

'The White Australia Policy ...'

'I think I just barely remember something about the
Chinaman when the girls took me to town with them on a
Saturday morning. They used to frighten me with stories if I
dawdled ... What he would do if he caught me ... You know
— a bogeyman. They had some rhyme they used to sing ...
Ching Chong Chinaman ... something rude, I suppose.'

'He would have been dead by then.'

'Well — they must have heard it ...'

'I wish I'd been older, I might have learned something,'
Tom said.

Caught out by the map, at nightfall they found their destination was a signpost, an abandoned fuel pump on a concrete
slab. The over-exposure of the abandoned site made them
uneasy; gave them the feeling that it would be naive to camp
there, alone, for the night. 'We'll go on,' Tom said. They
found a track that led off the road. In the last of the light
Tom skirted the area, collecting dry wood, looking for signs:
of who had been here, and why; of wildlife — of others. Out
of the confinement of the vehicle, perspective changed. On
the ground they were reduced immeasurably. The impact of
stillness and space affected them. Tom built a fire in the lee
of the truck, hiding the glow from the road. There was the
impulse to conceal, not to draw attention to themselves. In

the light of the gas lamp, Zoe prepared a meal.

Later, they spread the map out on the table. On either side of the artery of the highway with its thread of names, cutting across the blue filaments of rivers and wisps of mountains, were the angular sand-coloured excisions of Aboriginal land: oblongs and squares carrying names with conflicting consonants:Walamanpa-Walpiri Yingawunarri, Mudbara, Karlantipja Waanyigarawa, Wirliyajarrayi, Alyawarra, Pitjantjatjara. They stumbled over pronunciation.

'You can see what happened,' Tom said. 'Settlement pushing out from the east and the south looking for gold, land, water, whatever.'

'It's like a growth,' Zoe said. 'A lichen, spreading out.'

The pattern on the map was clear, the dense mass of names in the east, thinning out as they moved towards the centre. The sand-coloured oblongs of desert with their string of unpronounceable consonants were bare in comparison; places too harsh for the growth to take?

'A web of language, covering the surface.' She traced their route with her finger, thinking of the surveyors who had measured and counted the distance, walking the topography, feeling the wind blow along a valley, climbing a hill to find a trig point. Looking for water. She ran her hand over the map with its gridlock of signs. 'The names change nothing,' she said. 'Underneath the land is the same.'

'Some of it's changed.' Tom was a landholder. He knew what he'd had to do to make the land produce. The Ord dam. Kununurra ... the lush crops stretching out ... mining ... buffalo ... cattle. 'Changed forever,' he said.

'If there are original names for parts of it, there must have been one name for the whole of it?'

'Before it was mapped? Gondwanaland?'

'Where did that word come from? No. Before that ... I

46

wonder what the Makassans called it?'

'Maybe it didn't have one name, people just ... lived here,' Tom said, 'for how many thousands of years? Forty, fifty thousand years?' They looked at each other.

'Simple isn't it,' Zoe said. 'When you put it like that.'

Moths clustered around the hot white light of the gas lamp. Tom and Zoe went outside into the night. As the sky blazed over them, the curvature of the earth was visible. Temporarily, they were caught in the rapture of stargazers. Night navigators making their solitary way. The map gave them no certainty. It was evidence of calculated measurement — nothing more; an artifice of ownership.

They made love in their narrow bed, holding each other against the loneliness of a strange terrain, knowing the pathways in the dark, the angularity and concavity, the fold and flow of body, by touch.

Zoe woke in the night, unsure of where she was. This is what it is like to be homeless, she thought, to wander, disconnected. Without signposts. Belonging nowhere. Afraid of emptiness. And the silence: prescient and powerful, pushing down on them. They had only the clutter of their personal histories as bulwarks against uncertainty. Stirring the memory, causing dreams in the night's hiatus from the journey towards the centre.

> 'Tis a bitter change from those gay days that now
> I'm forced to go
> And must leave my bones in Santa Cruz far from
> my own Mayo

Athol Madden, her father, had been a great one for quoting. And stories — always with the defeated, bitter end. Grief and anger. Restlessness. And for what? God knows.

The unknown, lost place? His brother Aidan had been the same. Aidan had been the singer. Those sad sentimental songs that everyone knew. But when he sang 'The Snowy-Breasted Pearl' or 'The Harp That Once Through Tara's Hall' you could hear a pin drop. Other songs ... the music lost, only the words and the tune passed down. How the women of the family had loved those men ... and indulged them. They had needed them. There were no explanations. No one spoke of the source or the connection to other places; no one knew where they had come from — or why. About that there was silence. The songs and the stories were remnants that held them together. The repetition, the cycle of family celebration, had bored her as a child. Still, there was something in it. It could reach out and claim you. A loneliness of the spirit. When the mood was on her — the melancholy — she could not be dissuaded from it. And then, she might wonder about the silence, what it concealed. And those she might have asked were all dead.

Ellen Madden

She had watched the coast. A smudge, gradually becoming a distinct line, stretching along the horizon. Then the white break of waves. The air was soft, and the sun — a warm balm on her skin — raised the smell of damp and mildew out of her clothes. There was a tang in the wind pulling at the reddish-brown hair twisted up in a knot. She breathed it in, a wood smell, sweet and smoky. There were patches of clear green water now and then, and she could see down into it, see there would be an end to it. The terrible sea, the terrible rolling endless lurch of it. Land. Any land. No matter how barren or ugly ... Away from the sea. She would never want to see it again.

She was a tall woman. She held herself straight, her knuckles white on the rails against the ship's roll. The face was set. Closed. Only the eyes, if it had been possible to look into them, would have revealed something. Brown. Deep-set. Dark-lashed. The residue of strong emotion had pooled there. She stood apart from the other passengers. Unapproachable in her composure.

With the small white body, the tiny wan old man's face wrapped and sewn into its canvas shroud, had gone the last of her innocence. Gone. Over the side. When Dennis had taken the bundle from her — and consigned it to the deep — a scrap, a nothing — she had let go. Faith, belief, hope? Call it what you like, she had seen things for what they were. There was no going back. The old were dead and the young were dead and nothing would change that. No priest's words changed that. It was not the priests who died — of cold and hunger. Although they lived poor enough, God knows. No — it was the old and the young, buried in the rain-sodden ground. She was not an animal to work in the fields, up to her waist in mud. Broken and bent before she was thirty. Or a servant. She was that rare and useless thing in Ireland: an educated woman. 'What can we teach them that does not add to their despair?' she had asked her father in the cold room where he gathered his pupils. 'Ignorance will not save them from despair,' he had told her. Anger flickered inside her, warming her blood. It was the anger that would keep her alive. At Queenstown harbour, in a gloom of fog and rain, she had left her family. In Liverpool, when the ferry docked, she had seen what it was like there: the same cold poverty, the contempt that greeted them, and with the child already inside her she had said to Dennis, 'I will not wait here.' And yes, it was her. She had done it. She had gone against him and with the last of their sovereigns bought the first passage to Australia she could find. And the child had died.

With the terrible storms and the endless retching and no proper food to eat herself. And the captain daily eating his porridge awash in goat's milk. She had gone to him and seen it for herself on the table. With her hair down and her garnet brooch and her bodice soaked with eau de cologne. She had asked for milk for the child. 'To save its life,' she had said. 'No,' he had told her. 'If I give it to one I must give it to all and there is not enough. It would cause trouble.' 'She'll breed another soon enough,' he'd said to the officer sharing his breakfast table. She'd heard him say it. She had looked into his eyes and seen that there was no feeling there. To him, she was a creature of no value and she had cursed him and his kind, and his progeny if he had any. Perhaps he had seen the red glow of her rage because he had turned away from her. She had refused to let him perform the burial. 'Dennis must do it,' she said. They had thought perhaps she was mad because of it. But they were wrong. She was cold and strong and clear in her head. She would have other sons. And they would want for nothing. Land ... freehold. With her own name on the deeds alongside her husband's. Beholden to no one. No Englishman would cross her doorstep without her say so. That is what she would have out of this place.

She held tightly to a red and gold painted biscuit tin as Dennis helped her into the whale boat. In the tin were the few things that recorded their existence. Their marriage certificate, the scraps of paper that said they had paid their passage on the Sulphur with Captain Hamilton, and the letter that said James Edmond Madden, an infant of six weeks, had died at sea. There was the letter she had written to her father and mother and the garnet brooch. There were needles and thread and a silver thimble that her grandmother had given her. There was a lace handkerchief that her mother had woven for her and a pair of black kid gloves.

She put up a hand to shield her eyes from the harsh morning light. She could see the white beach stretching away and the huddle of low white buildings. Beyond, there was a faint smudge of blue hills. The boat nudged aground. As Dennis helped her ashore she swayed against him, the white sand rolling under her. The white buildings lost shape, flowed into the sand. Above, the enormous blue arc of sky tilted, enclosing her. In the incandescent blaze of blue and white, in the strange and alien hallucination of landfall, Ellen Madden was pierced by loss. It was not home. It would never be home. Never, never again would she be home.

51

The Middle Way

On the Way

On the way to Mataranka they turned off the highway. Zoe, who was reading the map, was sure she was right. Ten kilometres in was an *Historic Pub*. The road quickly deteriorated into a narrow track, water-rutted and stony. There was no possibility of turning around. The campervan swayed dangerously as they climbed in low gear up an incline that had seemed slight when they started.

In the short space of time it had taken to turn off the highway everything had changed. They had been lighthearted. Now Tom was concentrating on keeping the vehicle on the eroded track and Zoe was silent and anxious. She didn't know how capable he was in the situation. She put a hand on his thigh, feeling the muscles flex as he changed gears, ashamed of her self-concern.

The road crested the incline and levelled out. They were on a narrow plateau. Tom stopped the truck and got out, walking back to the edge of the track. 'No one has been up that for a long time,' he said.

Ahead of them was a cluster of corrugated iron buildings. As they drew near, the buildings resolved into derelict sheds, rusted iron loose and flapping in gusts of wind. A hand-painted sign on a piece of tin propped against one of the walls read: *WWII Museum*. An arrow pointed ahead.

'There must be someone there,' Zoe said, unwilling — now that they were safe — to concede that she had misread the map.

Grey cloud drifted across the afternoon sun, and in the flat metallic light the landscape lost dimension. The track descended through breakaways of blackened scrub, contorted extrusions of sandstone piled and tumbled down the slopes of the mesa. It led them to a large hangar on the edge of a bare plain stretching to the horizon.

'It's an old airstrip,' Tom said. 'A big one.'

Zoe wound down the window. 'There's no one here. No sign of anyone.'

They parked near the hangar and walked over to an opening cut in the corrugated iron. In the dim light inside they could see pieces of torn and twisted metal on the floor. The fuselage of a large aircraft, spattered with corroded holes. The shattered metal was shocking. In the eerie emptiness of the hangar it shrieked death and violence at them. Tom walked around, touching the metal, peering into the interior. Zoe stayed back, unwilling to make a connection. For her, World War Two was a text, a film, a documentary, a memory of events on the periphery of her life: the air-raid shelter her father had dug in the garden and on which her mother had planted coxcombs. Flowers had grown exuberantly in the excavated loam.

Zoe wandered around the perimeter of the hangar, examining the work benches. She made little sounds of distress at a dusty photograph pinned to a board. A group of young men, laughing. A faded typewritten account:

John Harvey 21yrs Allan Wright 23yrs Robert McKinley 21yrs and Kevin Sullivan 24yrs of the 35th squadron of the RAAF died of their wounds in February 1945. These young men risked their lives to transport supplies to Australian troops in the jungles of New Guinea.

On a return flight they were pursued by Japanese zero fighter planes and were hit several times. Pilot Kevin Sullivan was killed outright and his co-pilot, Allan Wright, was mortally wounded. John Harvey, radio operator, and Loadmaster Robert McKinley brought the aircraft back despite their own severe wounds.They died of their wounds shortly after landing.

They had been so young ... Not knowing anything about life. Dying for an idea of country which existed in their imagination, not this hard bare plain — this no-man's land.

'It was a DC3,' Tom said, beside her. 'They were unarmed.'

On the benches were trays of rusty washers and bolts. Hanging from a nail was an immersion heater, enamel mugs lined up below it. A pair of wire-rimmed sunglasses swung blind from a hook. Someone was keeping it like this — as though it hadn't ended ... as though a glint of metal would appear in the sky and then the drone of engines. And the boys would be back safe, laughing and joking. A pair of torn overalls hanging from a peg waited for the owner to flesh them out.

The wind rolled a drum against the outside wall. It knocked steadily. When Tom stood the drum upright he saw a rough slit had been cut in the top. *Donations for the museum would be appreciated* was stencilled there.

Tom walked out onto the broken surface of the airstrip, absorbed.

'Let's go,' Zoe called him. 'Let's get out of here.'

He waved a hand. 'There must be someone around,' he called back.

Suddenly she was infuriated. 'It's abandoned. Can't you see. Everything is dead and ruined. We shouldn't be here. Something has happened.'

Tom walked back. 'There's been a fire.'

But the emptiness attacked her, sending her messages in the prowling wind. There was a horror in it. 'Tom,' she pleaded.

In the truck, with the motor running and Tom beside her, Zoe felt foolish. The road continued past the hangar and around the base of the mesa. They drove on into a thicket of brush and tall grass crowding the edges of the track; signs of water. Ahead of them they could see the fronds of a date palm and ... roofs. Two rundown houses. Close by was a mud-brick building so low it seemed to be subsiding into the ground. A rough bough verandah had been built on to it and a sign wired to a pole read *Adelaide Springs Hotel 1912*. They laughed. The *Historic Pub*. 'I'll buy you a drink,' Tom said.

Zoe followed Tom through the low doorway. At first glance it looked ordinary. Rows of bottles behind the bar. Glasses. A blackboard price list of drinks on the wall. A man came from a back room and served them cans of lemon squash without conversation. Tom broke the silence. 'We've just had a look at the museum. Does this road lead back to the highway? We came in the other way,' he added. The man nodded, wiped the counter. He dropped their coins into an old metal till and returned to the back room. They sat on uncomfortably high stools, against the bar which came to shoulder height.

Zoe went out to the verandah to find a toilet. When she came back she whispered to Tom: 'Let's go.'

'What was all that about?' Tom asked when they were driving.

'Didn't you notice? There was about two inches of dust on everything. And ... the toilet was weird.'

'How?'

She tried to explain. 'The toilet was only about a foot off the floor, you know, like a child's toilet, and it had an overhead cistern ...' Tom looked at her. 'The chain to the cistern was so high I couldn't reach it. It was all out of proportion. Like the bar ... The right pieces put together in the wrong way somehow. And there was a woman out there, in one of the rooms. I went to speak to her and she ducked back inside. But she was watching me, I know.'

They drove at a slow pace along the barely discernible track. At times, looping around outcrops of rock and detouring deep mud ruts, the truck swayed and jolted. 'God knows where we are, I've lost all sense of direction,' Tom said. The sun, hidden behind the heavy cloud cover, offered no point of reference. He checked the gauge. 'We're getting low on fuel.'

Zoe wanted a caravan park, other people. Food and a hot shower. 'I won't use that map again, it's misleading. We could end up anywhere.'

It was late afternoon when the track intersected the highway and near nightfall when they reached a rundown fuel stop with a few caravan bays behind it. Tom pulled in, the gauge showing empty. Zoe listened to his conversation with the attendant.

'Do you know that old pub out there?' He gestured west.

'Nothing out there that I know of, mate,' the man replied. 'They say it used to be good cattle country once.'

'I thought there was a World War Two airstrip around here somewhere.'

'I wouldn't know. I've only been here three months.'

You never knew what to believe, Zoe thought. It was as if people didn't want to admit that there was anything beyond the boundary line of the highway. The noise and lights of the fuel stations and caravan bays were familiar constellations. Everyone made for them; known navigation points fixing their position. Her mind jumped to how long it would be before they could turn for home, the safe cushioning of family life into which they could sink, vanish if need be.

In the sultry darkness sleep was difficult. A man was playing an accordian in the caravan next to them. A grab-bag of old songs. Everyone knew them. No one knew where they came from: 'Mexicali Rose', 'Lambeth Walk', 'Beautiful Dreamer'. Zoe had seen him, a slight man, ride up on a bicycle. His caravan had been closed and in darkness. He'd knocked persistently on the door and then the windows and walls of the van, calling to whoever was inside. Finally he'd been admitted. Shortly after the music started.

'I wish he'd stop,' Zoe whispered to Tom, 'I want to sleep.'

'I was talking to him at the shop. He and his wife drove up the Tanami in that old Holden. He's seventy-eight.'

'Well, they should be home with their grandchildren,' Zoe said. 'What is he trying to prove?' She wondered about the wife who wouldn't let him in. Sometimes the crossed threads of strangers' lives bothered her. She couldn't get them out of her mind. Like the boys. Their faces laughing, their bodies seeping blood onto the floor of the hangar. Disbelieving their own death. Not ready for it. Something unfinished was trapped in that deserted hangar. Pain or fear. Forcing its way into the present. It was not history as she had supposed it to be.

The old man had exchanged the accordian for a mandolin and was playing 'Cielito Lindo'. God, what next. At least he wasn't singing. There was no sound apart from the music. No murmur of voices between songs. Nothing. What was the woman doing?

Zoe nudged Tom. 'Did you see the woman with the old man in the shop?'

'No,' Tom replied, without opening his eyes. 'He was buying a hamburger, in case you're interested.'

'How do you know his wife is with him?'

'Because I asked him if he travelled down on his own and he said: "Just me and the wife".'

'It's odd ... It doesn't seem as if anyone else is there ...'

Sweet and plaintive, the mandolin played 'Ramona'.

'He's performing,' Zoe said. 'He knows everyone is forced to listen. It's sad. Lonely ...'

'He's all right.' Tom rolled onto his back.

Zoe had fallen silent, her breathing light and even. Tom was careful not to wake her. The mandolin lingered over another tune. The old man had been buying his evening meal and had taken time over his selection of a hamburger, wanting to talk to whoever would listen. Tom had known men like him. Tough as old Harry. Fencers, shearers, itinerants. They turned up in the season. You could depend on them. Some of them, like the old man, had been talkers; they always knew what was going on around the bush. You'd never know if they were lonely. They haven't been around for years, Tom realised with surprise.

The music stopped. Everything was quiet. People went to sleep early and started early. When they got to Mataranka they'd stay a few days he decided, have a rest.

Mataranka

It was mid-afternoon when they reached Mataranka; they had learned not to arrive late in the day. Like tired refugees, the unending stream of caravans sought shelter at night. Latecomers had to take the worst sites. It was the time when tension broke through the skin of self-containment like a heat rash. The elderly fared worst. Tired after their day's travel, the irritations of unaccustomed intimacy became manifest: bodies — larger, thinner or less agile than they had realised — bumping into each other. Squeezing into too-small table settings. Bobbing heads to reach storage cupboards which spilled their contents when opened. Lifetimes of habit jarred by change. Rubbing thin.

Zoe waited in the truck while Tom went into the office. Mataranka was just off the highway between north and south, the two poles of Australia: the monsoonal heat and humidity of the tropics and the seasonal temperate south. In the north the continent spread, in fragments of islands and sand spits, into exotic seas and landscapes, merging in a thousand subtle ways into a lusher sensual world. Demons and gods of a different kind waited there in jungles offshore. In the south, placid green pastures came to a precipitous shocking end. An impetuous, not-knowing — one step too far and the body could fall, pulled into the void by the wind. Tumbling over and over, falling into a cold deep ocean. It was a paradox: the difference at either end of an arid centre.

Studying the map, Zoe saw that they had reached a point of convergence. The great circle travelling the perimeter of the continent was dissected neatly by the Stuart Highway — a diameter — cutting through the centre. Within the large circle there were smaller intense circles of habitation: the Kimberley, Arnhem Land, Northern Queensland. South Australia hugging the Bight. The fertile valleys and forest remnants of the south-west corner where they had come from. This was the point where decisions would be made: whether to go back or go on. To go up or down. To go around or slice through the continent in a compromise. The desert and the thin ribbon of road were tricky. Emptiness, irritation and boredom affected the travellers like sudden passing storms. On the horizon, mirages appeared and disappeared. With infinite indifference the landscape played on them; drawing them out, changing their minds.

Mataranka was another oasis. There were thermal springs; fronds of palm trees were visible above the lush tropical undergrowth of pandanus that hid the springs from view. It was not like the usual caravan park but was more like a settlement, a village. A complex of buildings huddled together.

Tom came out of the office with the clutch of paper that meant they were booked in.

'It's a big place, but they seem pretty casual. We can park anywhere down near the fence. It's a working cattle station as well.'

He dropped a sheaf of brochures in Zoe's lap: '*Scenic Bush Tours, Garden Bistro, Guided Tours, Horseriding, Elsey Homestead Replica*,' she read out. 'Did you know that *We of the Never Never* was filmed here?'

'The whole place looks like a film set.'

'And we're the extras,' Zoe added, 'for the crowd scenes. It's a coach tour destination too.'

The word 'destination' sounded wrong, misspelled or misplaced. A *Destination* was a significant endpoint — not a 'coach stop'. There were no real destinations, Zoe had discovered, only brief stops. In each place she had looked for something significant, a key that would provide an explanation. She had not found it. The point of the travelling seemed to be to keep going. To go around. In a fit of frustration one day she had said to Tom: 'There is no point in what we are doing.' It had upset him. 'I thought we'd waited twenty years to do this — see the country.' 'Yes, she'd replied, but *what are we seeing?* We only touch the surface. It's superficial. It means nothing to us. We drift ... '

'Stop thinking,' Tom had told her, but Zoe couldn't.

There were others who seemed to be waiting — for an explanation, or perhaps, even — a revelation. Out there, in the almost-overlooked stops, there was evidence of an exodus: things started and left incomplete. Buildings abandoned. Projects. Machinery. A road half-made, the road base left in piles as if an unexpected threat or a sudden overwhelming failure of will had occurred. Attendants watched over your shoulder while they served you food or fuel, their eyes on the horizon, glad to see you go. Their waiting was provisional. It was an interim existence, disconnected from the past. Wary of the future.

Tom wandered off when he had set up the van. The men sought each other out, gravitating into groups of two or three, glad of an opportunity to escape the swirl of emotion that accompanied arrival. They reaffirmed their separate existence in the talk of vehicles and horsepower and fuel consumption per kilometre, of road surfaces and routes. They offered the total of kilometres they had travelled as a qualification before they got down to the subtleties of establishing a hierarchy. Zoe sat in the van near the open window and listened, engrossed in the manoeuvres which would establish winners and losers.

Freed by the anonymity of the road, the men divulged details of their businesses, their jobs, the payout figure of their superannuation. They listed their previous journeys. In anecdotes they demonstrated their skill and superiority. They would stop talking to watch a new arrival back his caravan into a bay, how many tries before he got it right. If the wife got out to direct him it made it more interesting.

Some routes had a higher status than others: the Tanami desert track, the Strzelecki, the Gunbarrel Highway, the Gibb River Road. Sometimes a clear winner would come along. Like the young, carelessly confident man with an old Toyota four-wheel drive, its roof piled with dusty camping gear, who had been in Arnhem Land. They asked him questions, shifting their ground. Testing him. The names rolled off his tongue: Oenpelli, Maningrida, Nhulunbuy, Borroloola ... *He* was the traveller. *He* was the one. Powerful and free. Going to places beyond their reach. He was gentle with them, 'I travel by myself mate. Company slows you down.'

Zoe studied him, hidden behind her curtain. The thin

brown legs ending in crumpled socks and dusty boots. The hat, frayed and stained, hiding his hair and face, except for the sharp chin and wide thin mouth. He was familiar, although she didn't know him; he was a type she recognised. There could be no harm in him.

I would go with you, she thought. I wouldn't slow you down (the excitement of the silence and space stirred in her stomach, the energy ...).

The group lingered after the young man moved on. 'I'd have a go, but it's not fair on the wife,' one man said. The others agreed. It wasn't sensible. You could get into trouble out there. The next day they would be anxious to move on, covering their tracks, concealing, in their concentration on the mechanics of driving, their knowledge that they had waited too long.

The women gravitated to the ablution blocks. In the evening, while the northern sun — blood-red in a pale green sky — tinged everything with a rose light, they waited in lines. Toilet bags and hairdryers, clean clothes draped over their arms. They talked while they waited, always of the same things. The toilets and showers at other places, the hot water supply. They did not need to think about what they were saying. It was a series of utterances, an established entry into their own network. Sometimes, in oblique tales, they recounted events that had happened on the road. *He ... my husband ...* The women nodded their heads. *Men! They're all the same.* In the tone of their voice, the choice of words, they sought sympathy or solidarity while they had the chance. They gave and sought information: where to go, what to avoid. Some of the women listened without responding. Time and distance had had an effect. They had grasped the essential patterns that ruled their lives. It was here that they felt furthest from home. It was the lack of privacy for their needs, for the artifices and subterfuges they kept hidden. In some cubicles there were no hooks on which to hang their clean clothes, the wooden bench was wet, trailed with soap or talcum powder. The cellophane tabs from tampons were signs of the hot secretions of their bodies that *would flow*, waxing and waning in strange places. The older women were stoic and patient, acknowledging, in shy jokes, the unreliability of their hormones.

When they stopped for a day or two somewhere, the men attended to their vehicles. They would unroll a mat and have a look underneath, tightening and adjusting, making minor repairs. The women did their washing; their own bodies or the sweaty dusty clothes they carried with them from place to place. It was necessary if they were to go on. More important than food or sightseeing was the need to scrub out the red dirt that got into everything, for washing away the anxiety of displacement and restoring a veneer of control to their lives. The young mothers travelling with children were different, they didn't seem to worry about anything. Their bodies and their children's bodies were sleek with health. In the showers, the mothers and children chattered and laughed together. They came out one by one, fresh and sweet, causing a yearning in the waiting women which sent them trudging through the dust with their clean feet and a pocketful of change to telephone, to reconnect themselves to families who did not miss them.

'And how are the children?' they asked. 'How is the garden? What is happening? Tell us everything ... Yes, yes,' they would say, 'we are having a wonderful time.' They never said: We are tired and we can't stop, because if we stop we will never get home again.

The telephone calls made the women restless. The house, back there, with all the lovely things that they owned —

polished, clean, secure, over which they had control — glowed like a jewel in the mind; that was what they yearned for. They cleaned their caravans, placing mats precisely to catch the dust. They shook things and hung them out to air. They took photographs out of drawers and stood them, temporarily, on a shelf. When they were finished, some would put a chair near the caravan door and take out their knitting or crochet. They concentrated on their work, as if, strand by strand, they could construct an insulation against the strangeness of their surroundings. Sometimes they caught their reflection in a foreign mirror and were surprised. The grey had grown through their hair colour. The harsh light showed fine lines they had been unaware of. They would look away. No one knew them. They were moving on tomorrow.

It was at the laundromat that the women were most likely to lose their self-control. They came, sharp-eyed, looking to see which machines were clean, which were due to complete their cycle and whose turn it was next. It was not fair to use more than one machine, not fair to go away and leave the washed clothes uncollected. It was Zoe who took them out, one day, and put them on the bench. The owner of the clothes arrived and exploded into a rage. The scarlet face thrusting at Zoe with venom. When she passed the woman later she saw the signs: the caravan parked in the sun, with no clutter of articles around showing a comfortable settling in. The woman sitting on a folding chair precariously balanced on uneven ground, her face stony with misery. There was no sign of a vehicle. The man had gone somewhere on his own. It didn't do to push things. Not out here.

Aldo Guerini had decided to take a coach trip to Mataranka. Spend some money on himself. He had eighty-five thousand dollars in the bank and he was fifty-eight years old.

Hardened and smooth as a walnut after his thirty-five years growing pineapples and vegetables in the Queensland sun, he was comfortable now with the heat and the dust, but he liked the lush fecundity of the tropics. In all his years in Australia he had never found a woman he would marry. There had been many, in the towns and pubs around the bush, and on his trips to Sydney. He could not get close to the Australian women. The Italian women he met, the sisters and cousins and daughters of his friends, were country women, *paesane*, entrenched in the old ways. As time passed, he became too Australian to be satisfied with that. In his fantasies he loved blonde women with sleek long limbs wound around him.

Lately he had begun to think about having no sons to leave his money to. He had even thought of returning to his town, but who would remember him? Who would care? His days would be drawn out interminably, sitting in the piazza with the other old men, or playing bocce, talking about nothing. It turned in his gut like a knife, sometimes, that he had not got what he had wanted from this country. Despite his hard work and willingness to bury his heart and his blood in it. It had not taken him in.

He had made his decision on the spur of the moment, walking into a tourist office in Sydney. He'd chosen the Mataranka package because it included accommodation. There was a tavern, a bistro; maybe there would be good food. He might meet a woman travelling alone, like him. It was cattle country; in the Stockman's Bar, last night, he had talked and drunk with three stationhands, still in their high-heeled elastic-sided boots and wide-brimmed hats. Afterwards he had wondered if it was part of their job, to lean against the bar and lead the tourists on. He had stayed, sitting alone at a table, eating the barbecue and listening to the country and western band. The boys strummed their guitars and sang sad mournful songs about fathers who'd left them and women who cheated them. They are only boys, Aldo thought. Why do they make such sad monotonous music. What do they know about loneliness?

He toyed with the idea of asking the widow to join him. She had sat beside him on the journey from Sydney and told him about her life. All those years her husband had worked and all he had talked about was going around Australia. It had kept him going. And then — when he stopped work — he died. So — she'd sold the caravan and spent the money on the coach trip. Because all those years they'd been nowhere — what with the family and everything. And she wanted to see it ... Life was too short. As she spoke she had shaken her blonde curls and eased her back, thrusting out her chest in a tremor of breasts. She smiled at him, showing the gap between her front teeth, and offered him coffee from the thermos she refilled at each stop. 'Don't you think we should get some pleasure out of life?' Her flesh was ample and white. He liked that. He had closed his eyes, pretending to sleep, and inhaled the smell of her innocent unused skin, and been tempted.

He went to bed in his cabin, restless and lonely. Stirred by the drink, the music and the young women laughing in the soft night air. He wanted more; there was no passion in his life. He needed a strong, overwhelming passion to use up his strength. He did not want to be sad.

In the morning, early, he dressed in shorts, a light shirt and walking shoes. He made himself a cup of instant coffee, then went out, following the track down to the spring. He turned away when he heard the sound of laughter and splashing, having no wish to come on a party of young people enjoying themselves, perhaps swimming naked as the stockmen had told him the young backpackers did. His pride would not allow him to show his loneliness. Without thinking, he followed a path, watching his feet on the black mud hardened and smooth. The palms were dense overhead and the path became increasingly narrow; the pandanus crowded in, their serrated fronds grazing his bare arms and legs. The path led, in twists and turns, back to the stream with its clear pools thickly fringed by ferns. In some, the water was cool, in others a faint mist of steam coiled on the surface. He walked on. When he'd got far enough away from people he would go into the water. Kingfishers, in bright flashes, darted in front of him. He sat, hidden at a pool edge, to watch them. He gave up the path and followed the watercourse, looking for a place he felt like bathing in.

He took off his clothes and folded them neatly, hanging his watch on a branch. The water bubbled and rippled around him. Its warmth gradually penetrated to his bones, to fingers, knees and back, worn after the years of bending and planting. His limbs floated and moved in the buoyant water. Above him the palms were motionless, a criss-cross of lines blurring in the sunlight. The gentle warmth was per-suasive. Perhaps he slept briefly, his head resting on the bank. Coming to the surface, as if softened and detached by immersion, he was surprised to find an anger in himself. It was the anger of disappointment. He had not intended to spend his life working in the earth like a peasant. He had been a clever boy, grasping early the fact that he would escape his destiny and leave his shabby city and barren hills as soon as he was able. At sixteen he had sailed from Brindisi, not looking back. Passionate in his resolve never to be hungry, never to be beaten. To succeed.

He let the anger float away from him; drift, like his milk-white torso, in the water. Across the pool and down the stream he floated. He thought that he had come by chance to Paradise. The green crown of the palms wheeled above him into the sky, the exquisite comfort of the water, the brilliant orange flash and dart of the kingfishers. He was Adam. At the Beginning. He closed his eyes, resting in his weightless body; thinking of all the things he could do. He thought of the widow's willingness, her good-natured intention to enjoy life. He might yet give himself to this country. For the first time he felt himself to be in love with it.

The air on his skin chilled him after his long stay in the water. He dressed hurriedly, feeling energetic and ready to eat, having had no breakfast. Eager now to get back and be amongst people. To enjoy himself. There was no path, but unconcerned he decided to cut through the undergrowth instead of following the stream. He pushed into the dense growth, turning his shoulder into the serrated fronds, crunching underfoot the deep litter of dried vegetation that waited for the catharsis of ignition in a dry season; heading into the great swamp that spread out from the watercourse in a vast floodplain, until it ran out against the stony waterless escarpment.

Zoe and Tom sat outside to have breakfast. Their neighbours were a young couple in a campervan who kept to themselves. Tom had exchanged a few words with the man who told him that he'd found a deep pool, and knew a way to lure the barramundi out. It was an unusual season. The monsoons had failed. The vegetation was dry and the river had withdrawn to deep permanent pools in which the barramundi hid. The springs were unaffected; flowed, unchanging, five million gallons a day, never varying their temperature of 34 degrees Celsius. The tropical rainforest around them stayed lush and green.

Every morning, very early, the young couple went down to bathe. 'They've been here three weeks,' Tom said. 'He says he might stay here until the Wet next year.' Zoe felt a curiosity about the woman. Did she have no ties? No family to be concerned about? How could they afford it? She looked so serene and pleasant. Perhaps it was, for her, the perfect place; the place that everyone looked for. Zoe had noticed, without meaning to, without consciously watching, that the woman was quick and neat. She cooked a meal on a small portable barbecue, washed clothes in a dish each evening and hung them on a line between two trees. In the morning the clothes would be gone when Zoe went out. The campervan was in perpetual readiness to move; the restlessness, which took hold of travellers after a few days in a place and kept them moving, was missing. This couple had stopped. *But they continued to do only the things one did when travelling — as if they had fallen into a deep somnolence, repeating their last conscious actions.* Zoe blinked. Momentarily she felt a slippage in time, into that parallel continuum where nothing seemed ordinary.

Bemused by the crowd after their weeks of solitary travel, Tom and Zoe strolled through the clutter of caravans, vehicles and belongings. In a central space they came across a large marquee with a banner stretched over the entrance: *He turns a desert into pools of water, a parched land into springs of water. Psalm 107. Four Square Gospel Church. All Welcome.* Further along was a battered Winnebago covered in travel stickers and painted insignia: *Walking Around Australia for God.*

'How many does that make?' Tom asked.

'With a purpose? Five, I think. The girl cyclist, the gypsy wagon, the man with the wheelbarrow. Oh, and that strange man in his underpants leading the horses.'

'I expect to hear the drum of a boxing troupe any minute.'

Zoe laughed, pointing to a bus: 'There's a Tae Kwan Do club.'

They joined a guided tour, trailing a party of new arrivals: Germans, French, Japanese, middle-aged Australians. The guide gave them his own history along with the history of the Mataranka homestead. A country and western musician from Sydney, he travelled up each year to do the season. On the banks of Elsey Creek was the reconstructed home of Aeneas Gunn. He explained in detail how the film company had used ingenious methods to obtain an aged look on the timber walls and corrugated iron roof: 'The iron was painted with acid, it gives it that rusted, patchy look,' he told them. On the unlined timber walls inside hung household items, tools, harness straps. A few pieces of furniture were set out, the displays roped off. The group crowded into the small space, listening attentively to the account of making the film of the book. Zoe drew Tom's attention to an engrossed American with a video camera ... 'He's filming the story about the film about the ...'

'Ssssh,' he hushed her.

In a dusty compound, a few bough shelters had been erected. The guide was warming up: 'The Aboriginal people from around here came in and built these for us.' (The travellers leaned closer — this was what they had come for — contact with primitive blacks.) 'There's none living here now.' The tourists were allowed to handle the spears and throwing sticks, while he spoke in an intimate joking way about the old men's rights over the young women and the young men having to wait for a wife. 'Most of the fights were over women.' He never mentioned the trouble there had been getting the people off the station and out into the bush out of sight. No one queried his information on tribal customs, except a neat, middle-aged woman — a nun. 'Utter rubbish,' she said in a clear voice. 'I could tell you a story about what happened to the Mob from this place.'

The guide hurried them on. The tour was nearly over. The last stop was the Bushman's Camp where they could drink billy tea and eat damper, buy souvenir digging sticks and boomerangs and Akubra hats. 'Leichhardt, the explorer, disappeared around here somewhere,' (the Germans looked serious). 'They never found any trace of him.' It was a throwaway line while he ushered them to tables and benches. *Leichhardt Leichhardt. Here too?* Zoe stored it away ... a thread to unravel later. *Had he found the springs first, rested and restored the party before he went on? Searching.* 'But wasn't it further south?' she asked the guide, given courage by the nun. He changed the subject. Took a mug of billy tea and sat down. He had one more story to tell:

'We had a tourist lost out there in the swamp last week. You might have heard about it. We searched for three days. Those pandanus thickets cut you to ribbons. All we found were the remains of his shoes. A fire had gone through. The poor bugger must have taken them off when he got into a pool and the hot ash burnt right through the soles. I'll tell you, the butts of those palms are like knives. I wouldn't like to try walking barefoot over that country.' (The guide had timed it right, holding the attention of the group.) 'We decided the guy had perished and called off the search, then one of the helicopter pilots heading north on a mustering run spotted him, twenty-three kilometres away. He was lucky. He was heading further away from the station all the time. Never said a word to anyone when they brought him in. Ungrateful bastard. Never even thanked the lady from Bathurst who told us he was missing. Chartered a plane and flew out the same day.' The musician-guide was used to an audience — knew how to effect an ending. 'I leave you here,' he said. 'Watch out for snakes on the way back. They're bad this year.'

The tourists stayed in a bunch after the guide had left, unsure of what to do next. The musician-guide would sing to them that night, under the stars, of his loneliness, pain and hardship in the *outback*, his yearning for love. The illusion would stay with them for some time that they had touched a hard and dangerous centre.

In the shade of the rivergum sheltering their van, they sat on their folding chairs and watched new arrivals settling in. They recognised people they had met before on the road.

'It looks like everyone ends up here,' Zoe said.

'By the time you get here you're ready for a rest.'

'It's like a dream factory. It's got everything. Palm trees, springs, cowboys, *We of the Never Never*. Lost explorers. It's been made easy. Everyone gets what they want in one package.'

'Maybe that's why they stay. The real thing is hard to find.'

A thought niggled at Zoe; a possibility. 'Perhaps this *is* as real as it gets,' she said.

It was the fifth day. The young couple had gone. Without a word. In the morning the space was empty.

Each morning now Zoe and Tom walked down the path through the lush ferns and palms to the springs. They edged into a pool, the irresistable flow of the springs keeping them in constant motion. They drifted in the warmth; a languorous letting go. In the unnaturally clear water, bodies hung suspended, limbs waved against the current, like sea creatures, vulnerable appendages to the sun-weathered naked heads. Without the concealment of cosmetics, hats or eyeglasses, it was easy, somehow, to pick out the Australians. They lacked the definition of the Japanese or Mediterranean. In the unaccustomed closeness of the rock pools, the Australians were embarrassed at the accidental touch of strange bodies. In the spatial arrangement of figures bathing, Zoe thought, they made no identifying claim on her eye. Not at home in the landscape, their unease was reflected in their bodies.

Water was the alchemy. It was everything. In a desert country, water shaped the people who lived there. They shared it. They celebrated its sacredness in ritual. Weeks before in Katherine Gorge, in a rock crevice high above the limpid beauty of deep water, Zoe had found a handprint. Unobserved, she had fitted her hand to it. Covering the small faded record, cold against her palm. It was water that made the presence of Man possible. Strangers were the ones who killed for it. Spoiling the source. On the bus back to town she had listened to the driver describing the tensions between the tour operators and the Aboriginal owners. There was big money in the tourist trade. He had been blatant in his scorn of Aboriginal culture, his jokes causing an embarrassed silence in the bus.

And weeks ago, at Zebedee Springs in the Kimberley, they had skirted the Pentecost Ranges and driven over a gibber plain, a blue haze of heat rising off the stone. Walking through eddies of dust in the whirl of a searing wind, they had reached the filtered green light of a palm grove. In the deep cool shade, the sound of water falling into rock pools had been an unexpected absolution. An ibis, landing silently on its stalk legs, had regarded them and bent, with utmost grace, to drink. They had bathed in a pool, playing like children. Zoe had cupped her hands under a cascade and poured water over Tom's head. '*Ego te absolvo*,' she said, 'I forgive you.' It was the old child's game, playing the priest.

'For what?'

'For everything,' she said, smoothing the hair away from his eyes, holding his weightless body against her with a touch. Refreshed, they had eaten the bread and cheese and drunk the water they had carried with them, refilling their canteen at the spring. It was the Promised Land and it had been hard to leave.

Returning to the van after her shower, Zoe was handed a pamphlet as she passed the Four Square Gospel tent. 'Pardon me Ma'am,' the man said as he stepped out of the dusk across her path. She was too startled to refuse what he offered. Tom laughed when she told him about it. 'Got caught by the sales pitch did you?' She discovered the pamphlet in a pocket when she was doing some laundry: *I am poured out like water and all my bones are out of joint; my heart is like wax.*

That was the trouble with an oasis, Zoe thought. You could stay too long.

Marked in a thick red line on the map was the Barkly Highway. They would have to decide if they were going to Queensland. Clinging to a pandanus root at the edge of the pool, Zoe held Tom stationary beside her. 'Have you thought about it?' she asked him.

'Yes, I have. We can't be away from the orchard that long. We'd better go through the centre.'

'Yes,' Zoe said. 'Yes. We can go tomorrow.'

The Centre

On Larapinta Drive

They drove as slowly as the traffic would allow along the road into Alice Springs. *The Centre,* the mythical town, ringed by red ochre hills; the almost perfect geographical heart. From the remoteness of the south-west corner of the continent they had made their way here, travelling slowly over the contours of the land. They had crossed mountains, rivers, deserts and plains, and thought of themselves as seasoned. Succumbing to distance, they discovered the experience of detachment. As they had moved deeper into the continent, away from the tidal undertow of coastal life that pulls the gaze of island dwellers outwards, they had begun to focus on the immediate.

With the visitors' guide open on her lap, Zoe steered them through town and along Larapinta Drive to a caravan park. Past houses of provocative architecture built into the side of a hill. Winding around streets edged with brazen earthen footpaths and overhung with a light fresh greenness of foliage.

The park was large and busy, but they found a place, then went out again, eager to look around. Following Larapinta Drive out of town and heading west into the strong shadows of late afternoon, they came to Flynn's grave on a small rise in sight of the MacDonnell Ranges.

'This is it,' Zoe said. 'This is the place. Flynn of the Inland was one of my heroes.'

The grave marker was simple and unadorned. Flynn had wanted to be buried in sight of the Ranges. They stayed, unwilling to break the stillness, watching the phenomenon of rapid vibrant colour change: the violet mountains to cobalt, the rich crimson earth to magenta, cut by the white slash of a rivergum.

'I've grown up with this,' Zoe said. 'This is where the legends come from.'

'It's magnificent,' Tom agreed, 'a foreign country, isn't it?'

'Oh no, it's familiar — to me,' she said.

'You know how, when you're a kid, you have a special place in your imagination which is *The Place.*'

'No.'

'Tom! Didn't you ever have a special place?'

'Not that I can remember.'

'Didn't you daydream adventures? All children do that ...'

'I was too busy, I think. You know how it is. I can't remember.'

Burnt sienna earth had turned to umber and the mountains were an indigo shadow against the darkening sky. They drove back to the park, exhausted from the long day's travel, too weary to go through the motions of setting up camp. In the sharp chill of the night, Zoe went to sleep with her arm across Tom, holding him to her for warmth, but also because of the boy, who couldn't remember an imaginary world. What had filled the empty space?

Over breakfast Zoe brought it up again, pointing to the map. 'See, Lasseter Highway? Lasseter's Last Ride — lost in the desert. No one ever found the gold. *You* know Lasseter ...' she prompted Tom. 'Flynn of the Inland ... Lasseter ... and ... Namatjira ... the purple hills, the white gums, the red earth. Mysterious and beckoning.' She sipped her coffee, caught up in remembering. 'The other thing was Tuckonie — I haven't thought of that for years — Tuckonie and *The Search for the Golden Boomerang* — on the ABC — remember? Peggy Harvey and Tuckonie and their friend Jack, travelling around the outback in a caravan looking for the golden boomerang. Peggy was white and had "blue eyes and gold hair", and Tuckonie was a "clever Aboriginal boy", who used to get thought messages from somebody called Nimity when they were in trouble. You never listened to it?' she queried again. 'It was in the forties, during the war. I thought everyone knew about Tuckonie. What *did* you do after school?'

'I was outside, I suppose. I lived on a farm. There were things to do.'

'Chores, you mean? You must remember something? I remember it all so clearly. When I think of it now! Two children alone, except for Jack who drove the truck and protected them when they were in danger. The parents never interfered. Now and again Jack took Peggy home to visit them. Two eleven-year-olds wandering around the outback on a quest for a mythical golden boomerang. It was magical. And the theme music was Tchaikovsky's *Dance of the Sugar Plum Fairies*! No one used the didgeridoo in those days. I was given a picture storybook of the serial and there they were, the purple hills, the white gums and the red earth. And then ... we acquired a Namatjira print and I knew it was a real place ... I'm finally here.' Zoe topped up the coffee mugs. 'I can't believe it.'

She pulled back the curtains and opened the window. The strong unfiltered desert light flooded the small space. She sipped her coffee, regarding Tom over the rim of her mug.

'What are you looking at?' he asked.

'The light is different here,' she said. 'It shows us up.'

'The Argonauts?' she asked, still recalling. 'Jason and the Golden Fleece? I don't suppose you listened to that either?'

Tom shook his head.

'My sisters were Argonauts. When we arrived at the coast for the summer Dolly would stand on the headland at Bunker Bay, with her arms out, and shout: *Thálassa Thálassa*, the sea, the sea. It was the beginning of the holiday. Dolly, Sophie and Clare, they were all mad about the Greek legends. For me it was always The Inland. Then it was the news ... the music was ... *The Majestic Fanfare* ... The War —'

'I listened to that,' Tom said. His grandfather pushing him. Hurrying to get the cows out after milking, cleaning down the dairy, hurrying to get finished before the News. There was so much to do. He had to shut the poultry in and feed them, check the fence against the foxes, chop the kindling for his mother and always the tension, while they ate their dinner ... being careful not to scrape his plate, not to make a sound. His grandfather cupping his ear to catch the wavering sound — the BBC announcer's grave voice.

'I remember hearing the news that the Australians had surrendered on Crete. That's where my father was captured. At Rethimnon. We didn't know that then, of course.'

No one had said anything. That had been the worst part. His mother had cleared the table. His grandfather had rolled a cigarette and stirred sugar into his tea noisily. Around and around the spoon had gone, hitting the side of the cup, and he remembered he had wanted to shout at them ... 'Is my father dead? Well is he, is he dead?' During the time they had waited for news he grew used to the silence. He understood what the three of them were doing: suspending belief in the intolerable, denying it. Nothing had happened. They worked as usual. The farm work never stopped. His grandfather doubled the size of the winter vegetable garden. Together they worked in the orchard, pruning, weeding, burning up. They repaired the boundary fences: replacing rotted posts, tightening wire. They avoided each other's eyes. At school, he played harder. He was tough and moody. He stumbled into puberty with the belief that he held his father's life in his hands. If he faltered, if he doubted, just once, his father would never come back. The silence became a deserted plateau in his mind where he was safe from the burden of it.

'But he came back,' Zoe said.

Tom nodded. He'd come back, but he was never the same: a bad tempered stranger, disrupting the hard even plane of life on the farm, sucking up his mother's energy. Tom had been glad to escape to college. 'He was sick.'

To end the mood, they began to wash dishes and tidy up. They talked about what they would do first: head out into the MacDonnells or look around. Have a rest, clean up their gear ... They had lost the fresh early hours of the morning and with them the impetus to hurry. There was no need to hurry. They were staying.

Mid-afternoon they drove into the town to buy food and look around. The hills that circled the town held the heat in. Caught in the condensed traffic of people and vehicles, they escaped into the airconditioned shelter of a shopping mall. Its size and splendour were surprising. Finding a coffee shop, Tom and Zoe sat and waited for service, watching the crowd. The developers had planned for overseas travellers; at the imposing travel centre where Zoe had gone to get maps, the attendant ignored her, moving instead to greet tourist parties. Everywhere there were signs: *French, German, Japanese, Indonesian … spoken here*. Gold, pearls, sapphires and opals, the country's riches, were on display and — dominating everything — Aboriginal artefacts, art and design. In galleries, a profusion of woven baskets, didgeridoos, carved wooden figures, spears and coolamons were displayed amongst terracotta pots of pandanus and bamboo palms in simulated bush settings. The walls were crowded with paintings. The layers and lines of colours, the loops and swirls of fine dots and cross-hatching, seemed to shimmer in their own force field. The factor which held the scene in balance was money. Something powerful and unique had been brought to the marketplace. In the galleries where the paintings had price tags in the many thousands, a discreet hush accompanied the exchange of travellers' cheques. It was the quietness of profound cynicism found in the inner sanctum of serious selling. Unstated but understood, the knowledge that money buys everything.

Mediterranean genes, Zoe thought, listening shamelessly to the French couple ahead of them who were arguing in exasperation at the failure of the supermarket staff to understand them. They were elegant in their khaki safari gear, their skin had the smooth olive tinge of the European suntan. Zoe smiled at the woman, who gazed through her, not seeing. Outside the supermarket, a hired LandCruiser was parked against the kerb. Children waiting in the vehicle were calling

out: *Maman, je veux un bain, Maman, j'ai chaud ... Maman ...*
Zoe smiled at them as she and Tom walked past with their
bags of food. The children stared back without expression.

'They're not friendly are they?' Zoe waved anyway.

'They're here to see the sights,' Tom said, 'and we're not
one of them.'

'I feel invisible,' Zoe said.

On the drive back to the caravan park, they passed a line
of people straggling towards a ravine in the stony hills that
pressed in on the town. Old men, their beards stark white
against their black faces. Old women, carrying plastic bags.
The men were so thin ragged trousers flapped around their
stick legs in the gusts of hot wind. They walked slowly in
single file. In the swift transition from day to night, the dark
side of the hill was already losing definition. The people
vanished into the shadow.

It had been a while since Tom and Zoe had phoned home.
After tea, they strolled up to the phone box. Tom talked to
Jeremy who was caretaking the farm. Zoe listened, decoding
the news. Jeremy never missed a chance to get at his father
about subdividing the back blocks into hobby farms: *Make
some real money for a change ...* It always made Tom tense. Zoe
asked about the children, the garden. She was told that
magic mushroom spore brought back by Bali trippers had
got loose in the district and the local mushroom farm had
been closed down. National television crews had been in
town. Lyle Colvin, the mayor, was trying to get rid of the
commune in the high hills again. Rotary had organised a
picnic field day to find and destroy mushrooms because of a
fear of hallucinations affecting the community. The
Agriculture Department said it was hopeless.

No, the children were not going mushrooming.

Yes, Jeremy and Liz were eating all the mushrooms they could find in the hope of a hallucination ... *There could be money in it, Dad ...*

'Tom, he's teasing you. Why do you take the bait?'

'It's time they got rid of those parasites. They've never done a day's work in their lives.' It worried him. The land ... The orchard ... *Dad, there's no future in it. Last year you had to bury your entire apple harvest ...* It was not straightforward anymore. His stomach gave a nervous flutter.

Zoe said nothing. She had been up there, in the treeline. Driving down forestry tracks and hiking through the bush to get a view over the valley she wanted to paint. She had come on them without warning. Amongst the rocks on the edge of the escarpment. The man had been playing a flute, a wavering sweetness. He had stopped playing and both of them, the man and woman, had regarded her with a slight amused smile on their faces. *She* belonged. *They* were the *interlopers*. But Zoe had felt like the intruder. They had gone, while she stood there, merging back into the thick bush.

Afterwards, she had wished that she had spoken, asked them where they camped, what it was like ... She had seen others like them in the town, cashing welfare cheques to buy food, so they had *some* money. But it was the thought of it: living wild and unruly, on the fringes of ordinary life. Sometimes a wisp of smoke from their fires would stain the clear sky. It infuriated Tom. 'The bastards will burn us out one day,' he'd mutter. She was aware of them, up there on the escarpment in the trees. Watching her go about her life. She had wanted to go back but hadn't dared. They had the dangerous fascination of difference.

They took a detour walking back to the van. Groups were barbecuing a meal, exchanging travel talk. Zoe called in at the laundry to see if it was busy. The German students she had met the day before were there again, using it as a place to read and make coffee.

'They're from Munich,' she told Tom. 'They want a lift out to Hermannsburg.'

'We can't take them,' Tom said. With the unit on the back of the truck, there was only room for the two of them.

'I know, but it would be interesting to see what they thought about the German missionaries and the country.' For months she and Tom had had only each other's company. Sometimes she missed the talk, the contacts she had made at the new university campus in the rural city near their farm. She had begun, tentatively, to read history, to resume painting; to move beyond the closure of the valley which had absorbed most of her life. She knew it had something to do with the man and the woman living free in the hills, but she had not wanted to question it.

They spent several days sightseeing: Simpsons Gap. Standley Chasm. The Ghan Railway Museum. The Royal Flying Doctor Service Base ... The sights around town. Waiting patiently in queues with other tourists. The disposals store in a side street off the mall, jammed with equipment for going bush, was the signal to think of moving out into the Ranges.

Tom went on a balloon flight, a notion that made Zoe's head reel with vertigo. She stayed behind, looking forward to exploring on her own. Across the road from the caravan park was a complex of buildings set in a large area of trees and shrubbery; an art centre and gallery.

She took her time, walking into town, going first to a pharmacy. 'What do the local women use to stop their skin drying out?' she asked. The clear desert air was so dry, the sun so endlessly hot, she could feel her skin creasing like tissue paper. She bought an oversize bottle of moisturiser and a larger hat, then sought out a bookshop. History was on her mind. She browsed along the shelves, and found what she was looking for: Hermannsburg and Strehlow, Albrecht, the German Lutherans ... the improbable convergence. Why had they come *here, to this desert and these people?* Namatjira — the celebrated icon — in biography and illustration. And after Namatjira, the new art movement *rippling through the desert in an unstoppable wave* she read on a dust jacket. She bought what she wanted, using her credit card, ignoring the cost.

Zoe made her way through the crowded hustle of the marketplace in Todd Mall, looking for a place to sit and eat her lunch while she looked at her purchases. Behind the Mall, in the pale sand of the riverbed, dark-skinned groups sprawled and lolled in a midday torpor. A still life, in negative. Leached of colour and energy. She ate her sandwich and watched a covered police van make its way slowly along the riverbed. Two khaki-clad policemen got out and extricated a figure from the group. From where she sat she could see the figure, loose-limbed, going without demur, his departure causing only a temporary ripple of movement in the rest of the group. At the caravan park they had heard stories about the violent fighting and drunkenness in the riverbed. 'Don't go there,' they were warned. 'It's dangerous.' In the blue heat haze refracted off the encircling ironstone hills the air trembled, a manic distortion of reality in which the extraordinary had become commonplace. *There was an imbalance at the centre.* She thought of Tom, above her somewhere. What kind of seamless remote overview was he getting up there? Drifting in a bubble of silk. She stowed the books in her backpack and,' under the shade of her new hat, began the hot walk back through the streets to the Art Centre.

Zoe wandered through the deserted pathways of the garden, looking for an entrance into the complex of galleries and theatres. In the main area a retrospective exhibition of Papunya Tula paintings was on display. In the airconditioned elegance of the foyer she found a sofa and sat, grateful for the cool air. She felt sweaty and dusty, unready to look at the paintings. The building seemed deserted. The reception desk was unattended. Hesitating, she pushed the heavy bag of books and her hat behind the desk. In the rest room she washed her face and combed her hair, brushing at her shirt where it was stained pink with dust. It was the best she could do.

In the quiet pure space of the gallery, lit by muted sunlight, the energy and power of the paintings had an overwhelming force. In their austere beauty, the authority of geometric forms and subtle earth tones, the underlay of pointillist dots and overlay of ideograms, were visually stunning. She hadn't known such master works existed. On an end wall a panel stretched across the space; an abstract depiction of a world of intimate knowledge of country. She walked closer to read the details: *Napperby Death Spirit Dreaming*. A spirit journey through the Napperby district. The painter, she saw, was dead — at forty-five. What kind of man, or men, out of what place, out of what life, had created such a painting? The complexity of mythology, spirituality and history in the landscape she and Tom had been travelling across confronted her.

A lone attendant appeared and Zoe bought a catalogue. 'I had no idea ...' Zoe said.

'Most people haven't,' the attendant said. 'They don't get past the dealers in the mall. We'll never see these again. They're on their way to New York.' She pointed to the introductory essay in the catalogue. 'That explains some of it ... about Papunya Tula.'

Zoe continued on. Painting after painting; bewildering in meaning, clear in expression of intent: an intricate coded rendering of a People in communion with their environment. *In these paintings was the balance.* In another room the psychedelic colours of other artists, their sense of eagerness and release in translating form onto canvas leapt at the viewer.

Zoe reclaimed her things and went outside. She was exhausted by what she had seen. Finding a place on the spiky, lettuce-green grass under the sparse shade of a tree, she read about the beginning of the movement at Papunya, Lajamanu, Yuendumu and Balgo Hills; the incandescent fire of creativity that had burned, first, in the old men, discovering a way to express part of what they knew. The world around her seemed flat and without definition. The shallow hold Europe had on the continent, the lichen growth of foreign place names that covered the surface, was a temporary usurpation. *We have missed the point*, she said to herself. Concealed by the curtain of leaves, through a filter of green, she watched the activity opposite, separated by the red earth verges of Larapinta Drive from the caravans arriving and departing. The stream of sightseers bought fast food lunches from the kiosk, filled gas bottles and bought fuel, engrossed in the minutiae of their holiday. She could find no connection between what was held immutable in the gallery and the diorama across the road.

Zoe was aware that she had undergone a change — a shift in perspective. Like grief; it was hard to grasp the dimensions of what she felt. It was the enormity of what had been lost: the wholeness of a people, the fragmentation of their world. The men and women at Papunya had kept it inside them, held on to it. *Papunya was filled with twilight people,* Geoffrey Bardon had written of his days there, *a quiet, desperate place of emotional loss and waste, with an air of casual cruelty.* And then the glory — *the conflagration,* he'd called it. Ghosts, phantoms, walked through her mind, disappearing in a silent line into the hills. The groups of figures in the riverbed, the drooping bodies lying entangled in the sand, were tableaux of displacement. Faces in the mall, fixed in stoic indifference, were faces she'd seen before: the black and white despair of Kathe Kollwitz drawings; the refugees of war. The images were European. But what other reference could she have? She didn't know these people. Didn't know the man who, with wry humour, had offered them the crudely formed boomerang outside an imposing gallery. They had bought it for twenty dollars in an impulse of solidarity with him. Along the way, the groups sitting under shade trees on the margin at highway roadhouses, or disappearing into the Long Grass at Katherine, were strangers. That's their address, the contemptuous bus driver had said. They live in the 'Long Grass'. And before that, the screams and shouts of anger in the night that had frightened her in the Kimberley. It had begun there, she thought. But no. Even that wasn't the beginning. There were ghosts on the boundaries of her childhood. Presences. Shadows. A silent complicity.

Zoe rested for awhile, until the ants found her and the increasing heat drove her to move. She walked through the garden to the impressive desert architecture of the Strehlow Research Institute, wondering what would she find here? The entry led the visitor from the bright daylight down into a darkened gallery. Spotlights illuminated blown-up photographs of Aranda people and the early Lutheran missionaries. Aboriginal artefacts were displayed in corners. The warm earth tones of the walls and the shadowy illusion of the interior worked on the imagination. A man appeared, gathered the small group of visitors and led them through a description of weapons and tools. He skilfully avoided personal questions from an American, and played the black warrior for the children, brandishing a nulla-nulla, showing them with a downward thrust how it was used to kill a man. He looked at his audience, invoking, deliberately, his connection to savagery. He thanked them for coming.

To Zoe's inquiry at the reception desk, the woman was courteously dismissive. 'There is no one here at the moment who can help you,' she said. Zoe wandered around, finding that the galleries and downward stairways led to closed doors, that in fact there was nothing to see. Whatever was behind the doors, or below in the vaults, was locked away. She persisted, waiting at the inquiry desk for someone to respond. What remained of the Strehlow collection of Aranda ancestral and cultural objects, she was finally told, was in the vaults, the subject of litigation.

They were packed up and ready to leave at first light, but Zoe couldn't settle. Tom, resigned to sleeplessness, said 'You might as well get up and make a cup of tea.'

She sat at the minuscule table, wrapped in a blanket, waiting for the kettle to boil. The desert nights were cold.

'What's the matter?' Tom asked.

'I just can't sleep.'

'Are you missing the family?'

'No. I haven't thought about them. It's not that.'

Tom was patient. 'What is it then?'

'It's the Art Centre, across the road. I went there today. I can't stop thinking about it. It's changed the way I see things.'

'That sounds dramatic.'

'I'm not being dramatic. The paintings — from Papunya, the master paintings. I don't think I could ever try to paint landscape again.'

'Oh, come on ...'

'No. I'm serious. We only ever paint the surface ... because we can only know the surface. While they ... work ... from the inside out. I don't understand it. They *know* the land and their place in it so completely they paint *the idea* of it. There is no separation ... They're in it. No horizon, no perspective ...'

The kettle boiled, hissing steam. Zoe turned off the gas jet and made coffee, spilling sugar.

Tom reached out for his mug. 'I don't know what you're talking about really ...'

'There is this huge gap between what they understand and what we see. How are we supposed to live in this country? After what we've done. Are we supposed to pretend that nothing happened? We know what happened. The more we see the worse it gets. It was a war, Tom. It still is. Everywhere we go we see the evidence of it. Now it's a war over what's left of their culture. Even their spirituality ... Fighting over the spoils.'

'It's history. It's happened in other countries. To the victor go the spoils. You can't change it — it's almost the year 2000, for God's sake. It's the past —'

'But we deny it. We pretend ...'

'What would you do? Give it all back? Aussie go home!'

'Where's home?'

'Home is the valley. I was born there. My father was born there. My children were born there and I'm staying there. Until I die. Jeremy will probably sell it after that.'

'I'm not attacking you ...'

'Yes you are, indirectly.'

Zoe couldn't let it rest. 'How did your grandfather get the valley anyway? You've never told me —'

'I don't know. He pegged it because traces of alluvial gold had been found I think. Maybe that came first. Later he planted the orchard. What's wrong with that?'

'Look. It's not what I mean ...'

'Well, what do you mean?'

'I don't know. I mean that ... terrible things have happened in this country, they happen now and ... we don't acknowledge it. We call it by other names. Or we stay silent. On top of that, we have the gall to take over their Aboriginality and flog it in the marketplace. I mean ... what would this place be without Aboriginal culture? What would the tourists come to see?'

'The Rock.' He was half-serious, half-mocking.

'At least they've got that back.'

'Who gets the profits from that I wonder?'

'Why is it all right for others to make a profit and somehow wrong for them? Why does it always come down to money?' Zoe pulled the blanket around her shoulders. 'I don't want to talk about money. Do you see what we've done? We can't talk about it — even to each other. Everyone avoids it.'

'Perhaps the country isn't ready for it,' Tom said.

'I'm ready for it.' She was sharp.

'You're out of your depth Zoe.'

It was no use. They would end up arguing past the point

of recovery. Silence was safer.

'Come to bed,' Tom said. 'We're supposed to be leaving in a few hours, for your magic country.'

Zoe dumped the coffee mugs in the sink with a clatter.

'The Golden Boomerang. How ironic — or prophetic. We don't belong here. We never will. Not like they do.'

'Maybe not, but we have to live with that. We've got nowhere else to go.'

The Sleeping Woman

The land was in shadow; a sombre brown slashed here and there with the russet of bare earth. On either side of the sealed road, and ahead of them, the MacDonnell Ranges rose and flowed in rounded undulating shapes, soft blue in the early morning light.

In the warmth of the truck Zoe listened to the cello concerto, the sound playing into her head via the headphones, shutting out everything except itself and the landscape. She had rummaged through the cassettes, looking for something that was right. Everything was too complicated; the complex refinement of the music wrong for the place she was in. It had to be a wind or string sound. A single resonance. Voice. What *was* the music of this landscape? The sound that would let you in. There had to be something. The cassettes were old, the classical canon brought from home; a curtain of sound through which her world was filtered. It had never failed her before. But now she needed a conduit — of her own making. In the end, she chose the cello concerto; Elgar's search through a tonal landscape.

Everywhere she looked now Zoe was aware of the imprint of the people who were bound up in the country. They were alien to her but she felt the collective power of their presence. What is happening to me? she wondered. She and Tom were voyeurs, transients. Why then did it feel like a homecoming?

As the sun rose the mountains gathered colour, the blue deepening to violet, the wounds of bare earth strengthening to blood-red. She perceived the invisible coherent net which bound the country and the people into one. She understood the loneliness integral to her own being: the state of *being outside*. The cello searched through a minor key for its harmonic home, repeating the theme. Reshaping it in a different key. Steadily, rhythmically, they drove further into the ranges on the well-made highway. It would be the limit of their journey into the interior. Zoe sighed, a slight involuntary escape of breath. It was part of who they were and how they travelled: the limitations. They could not venture far off the road.

They stopped in a cleared space to stretch their legs and walked a little way into a grove of white-trunked gums. Subdued and separate.

'There is water everywhere around here,' Tom said. 'Underground.' He stretched his arms, easing cramped muscles. 'No people, no sign. No sound.'

'The silence shimmers,' Zoe said, reminded of the paintings. 'It comes at you in waves.'

'I needed this,' Tom said. 'Mountains must be in my blood.'

She poured mugs of coffee from the thermos, feeling the sun warm on her back. They walked a little further into the trees. A flock of sulphur-crested cockatoos screeched in protest at the disturbance. They resumed travelling, soothed by the unexpected moment they had shared. We are like children, Zoe thought. Lost children. We don't know where we are going.

When they reached a junction they stopped to consult the map and make a decision. Hermannsburg was closer, and Zoe had her reasons for wanting to see it. In her bag were the books she'd bought in Alice Springs. What had they made of it — the Germans — with their hard unyielding God? What had it produced — this clash of will and spirit?

At the approach to the settlement, cans and bottles littered the roadside. Tom and Zoe passed the sign which told them they had entered the Ntaria Land Trust and that alcohol was forbidden. Driving across the dry bed of the Finke River, they stopped at a small plaque on the roadside which commemorated Namatjira. This was his country they were passing through. It was a defined tourist path but there was a difference: it was someone else's land. They passed a supermarket, a fuel station, groups of people walking to the shopping centre, feeling conspicuous and intrusive in the campervan.

'They must want tourists to come,' Zoe said, 'or there would be signs ...'

'If it was mine I wouldn't let anyone in,' Tom answered.

To their right, in the distance, were clusters of houses; ahead of them were the whitewashed buildings of the old mission. They parked outside a fence of wooden stakes which partially enclosed the compound. It was Sunday. With the engine switched off the sound of voices singing hymns in the nearby church filled the space. They sat listening, the European melodies subtly altered by the natural tonal harmonies of men and women and children, their voices blending. The language was not English.

Long ago, some painful transformation had imposed itself on the ground. The hard bare earth which surrounded the old buildings bore witness to the strength of the impact, the passage of feet; the traffic of change. The severe angular buildings, and the massive hand-hewn timbers which supported them, were evidence of enormous endurance and will. The first Lutheran missionaries had taken two years to find their way here. Arriving in 1877, they had quarried sandstone and burnt lime for walls. From the valley of the Finke River they had cut desert oaks for timber and carted flagstones for floors. They had named the settlement Hermannsburg after the missionary institute in Germany which had sent them and commenced the long travail of dis-assembling an ancient way of life. They had begun by learning the language of the people they intended to change, prohibiting the practice of ceremony; disrupting the force which gave meaning to the Aranda universe.

'It's taken just over a hundred years to get the land back,' Zoe said, reading from an information brochure. She and Tom ducked their head to enter the small room where Carl Strehlow had laboured over his master work *Die Aranda und Loritja Staemme in Zentral Australien*. Untranslated into English even now. The seven volumes of Aboriginal culture and language had been published in Frankfurt and remained in Germany; an effective hiving off of knowledge.

On the walls were photographs and curios of the early life of the missionaries: the heavy bodies and solemn faces of Strehlow and Albrecht gazed out at all who came there. Authority, Zoe thought. Determination and ... obsession?

Strehlow had died a terrible death. Critically ill, hugely swollen and in acute pain, with his wife and son (who would have his own role to play) he had endured a nightmare journey by horse and buggy. Through the Dreaming sites of the Aranda people; the birthplace of their ancestral Beings. Down the dry riverbed of the Finke, through mountain passes and desert plains, in heatwave conditions, tended by the Aranda people he had lived with for twenty-eight years. Forsaken by his religious colleagues, he had struggled with his own God to accept the torments of his agonising passage to Horseshoe Bend. He died on the tenth day.

A tourist bus arrived and bodies filled the small dark rooms. A dining room had been converted to a tearoom where two Aboriginal girls were busily serving Devonshire teas. Tom and Zoe joined the queue. Tom was jocular, loading his scones with cream and, momentarily, Zoe thought she had found him. She had a rush of affection — and remorse that she was imposing on him the tensions of her own journey with its stops and gaps, its unpredictable detours. They ate and drank, seated at a small wooden table with a lace cloth, sipping their tea out of the remnants of bone china teasets, listening to the chatter.

The tour party, by arrangement, had been shown around the old manse which was being converted into an art gallery. They caught the curator as he was closing the building and persuaded him to let them in. The gallery was dedicated to Namatjira and, the curator told them, he was trying to recover Namatjira works to hang there. Politely they listened to his explanations: Rex Battarbee, the first watercolours, the gradual flowering of Namatjira's art. When Tom began to say that Zoe was a painter she jabbed him with an elbow.

'What's the matter?' he asked, when they were outside.

'I couldn't bear the way that curator was talking about Namatjira — patronising him. This was his country. His mind would have been filled with the vision and knowledge of it. And yet, he revealed nothing of that in his art. It must have been a great conflict for him.'

'He had his chance,' Tom said.

'Some chance.' Zoe was lost in her own thoughts. At the beginning Albrecht would have bought him paper and paints; then came the lessons from Battarbee — copying the teacher, producing paintings to be sold in Alice Springs along with the other things the mission collected for sale (even Tjuringa, the sacred boards). 'Battarbee showed Namatjira a technique,' she told Tom. 'A European technique. Even so, he made something of it. Once he started to produce he must have been under so much pressure.'

'From his family too. I read somewhere that when he had money his relatives wanted to share it. Same old story isn't it?'

'Who are we to judge. He gave us our first vision of the centre. It fascinated us and yet — we couldn't leave him alone. Every middleclass family in Australia had a Namatjira print on the loungeroom wall — opposite the flight of ducks.'

'We didn't,' Tom said.

'Well, we did. But we didn't have the ducks.' Zoe took a breath. 'I've been reading about him; he died at Papunya, in 1959, where the old men did the paintings of ancestral Dreamings in the seventies. They weren't allowed to leave, you know. They were all collected up and dumped there. Different tribes ... It was a terrible place. They were reduced to nothing and *still* they survived.'

'How do you know that?'

'It's in a catalogue at the Art Centre. You must read it. It's not just the paintings, it's Papunya. What it was like. And Geoffrey Bardon. He was a teacher there. Without him the paintings would not have been done ... *a great artistic and spiritual conflagration,* he called it, *an expression of a humiliated and repressed race suddenly told they could speak to their own feelings.* If Namatjira had lived ... Years ago I saw a linocut by Noel Counihan — Namatjira crucified. I thought it was ... an overstatement. But Counihan was right. Namatjira *was* the sacrificial victim. He paid the price — of thinking he might have been permitted to live in two worlds.'

'That's taking it a bit far isn't it?'

'I'm right. I know I'm right,' Zoe said, getting sharp. 'And Strehlow's son. They *trusted* him, the Aranda, made him custodian for all their secrets and sacred things. Strehlow and Albrecht spent sixty-odd years trying to prohibit their spiritual life and replace it with Lutheran Christianity and they couldn't. They couldn't ignore it either. Do you know where the remnants of their cultural records are now? In the basement of the Strehlow Research Centre in Alice Springs — while a fight goes on over who owns them.'

They were following a map and a numbered guide to the mission buildings. On the edge of the compound, unnumbered, was a large lofted building. The boys' dormitory.

'Look at the timber in those roof supports,' Tom pointed. 'There must have been some big trees around here.'

'All that hard work and German thrift and industry,' Zoe said, 'and what did they achieve in the end? The missionaries are gone, but the people are still here.'

'I don't see anybody working.'

'You don't get it — you reduce everything ... the Protestant work ethic.'

'Oh. I see. Wrong again.' He was sarcastic. 'And the

Catholics were different, were they? They got it right?'

'No ... No one has got it right. But at least ... I think *some* of them knew that it was spiritual; that the struggle was for spiritual power.' She was thinking of Beagle Bay — the church with its blend of Christian and Aboriginal symbols; the suggestion that some kind of synthesis had been attempted. Suddenly she and Tom were on dangerous ground and it was her fault — she had brought it up. It was the old argument. Them and us. The old bitterness. What it was to grow up Irish Catholic in a Protestant country town. She, who had gone over to the enemy when she married, knew it well. It wasn't just status or money, or even religious difference. It went deeper than that — and it has something to do with how I feel now, she thought, although I don't know what. 'I feel for these people,' she said, taking offense. 'I just feel for them.'

They had completed the circuit of the remaining buildings. The sky was black with the impending storm and the whitewashed buildings were in stark relief. Mount Sonder brooded over the deserted mission.

Zoe showed Tom the postcard she had bought. 'It's Mount Sonder, the Sleeping Woman.'

The tourist bus had gone and they were suddenly conscious of being the only visitors left. Tom quickened his pace. 'We'd better make a move. It might rain and we've got to drive over unsealed road.' They followed the track through the settlement, leaving it huddled in the lee of the mountain.

It didn't rain; they drove back to the highway and turned towards Glen Helen with the clouds piling furiously and the light fading. The old homestead, built on the edge of a river gorge, seemed settled and solidly attached. Behind a row of cabins, there was a small space for caravans. The surprise was a dining room in the homestead with the intimate comfort and excellent cuisine of a good city restaurant. They treated themselves to dinner and a bottle of wine and tried to resurrect their own intimacy.

'This country,' said Zoe, 'continually presents you with another paradox.' Earlier in the bar they had sat over a drink, watching several young Aboriginal stockmen play-acting for a group of intimidated tourists. Hamming it up with 'blackfella talk' and larrikin behaviour. At Glen Helen they were at the end of the line; Namatjira Drive, the sealed road, ended here. Beyond it, and around it, were the mountains — and the land was now Aboriginal land.

They were self-conscious, dining à la carte in their best clothes, far from the routines and habits which, over the years, become a substitute for intimacy. It was possible, Zoe realised, to live like that — in amicable estrangement — skirting the areas of incompatibility — avoiding risks.

'It's strange to think that we can't go on,' Zoe said suddenly.
Tom looked at her.
'This is the end of the road for us. There's nothing out there. No accommodation, no fuel stations. It just seems strange, that huge area, and we can't go there. This is where it stops.'
'We could, if it was necessary,' Tom said. 'We could equip ourselves, it could be done. But there is no reason for it.'
'Would you like to keep going? Just to go there.'
'Yes, as a matter of fact, I would. I'd like to go on my own.'
'Oh,' Zoe said ,'would you? I'd be game.'
He looked at her, mocking a little. 'You think you are, Zoe. But you stay inside the boundaries like the rest of us.'

Walking outside after dinner they found the night air chilling. A full moon lit the landscape, and the dark shape of Mount Sonder revealed itself again, the huge prone female silhouette draped in stone. Silent. Asleep. Beyond reach.

On the pretext of having a leisurely shower in private, Zoe gathered her things and walked back to the toilet block. The cabins were in darkness. Theirs was the only van on the small grassed camping area. A sure sign that they had moved outside the main caravan path. She had a sense of intense curiosity — excitement. Tom was right. She didn't transgress the boundaries; she had never been conscious of them — until now; the prohibitions and barriers. The journey they were making was prescribed for people like themselves. Timid travellers, for the most part, unwilling or unable to see. The truth is, we stick together because this country frightens us, she thought. It frightened our ancestors and it frightens us. That's what we have made of it.

She walked slowly up the entrance drive towards the road that led into the ink-washed landscape. What is there to fear she asked herself: stray cattle, a dingo, humanity? From the silhouetted mountain, the Sleeping Woman, she felt a benign calmness — and yet ... The surrounding landscape was charged with power. It called her. There was no other way to put it. In the neutrality of moonlight an interstice had opened for her. She walked towards the edge of a ravine, looking into the riverbed below. The air was intensely cold. She stood motionless. Listening. Was it in her head, or was she hearing it: that faint ringing sound, a vibration of sky and earth? The night waited for her. She unfolded her arms, hesitated, then raised them, letting the chill penetrate her body; stretching towards the mountains, the ravine, the sky. She crouched on the stony ground. I am in the centre, she thought. This is the centre. Drifting away from her, like the threads of her condensed breath issuing into the stillness, she saw how she had manufactured an existence; the expenditure of energy which moved her. She saw, with tenderness, the passionate illusory brevity of such a life.

Zoe followed the moon on its incline, walking a little way along the cattle pad at the edge of the ravine, careful of how she went. Had Albrecht come this way on such a night, on one of his long camel rides into the country beyond Haasts Bluff looking for the people who lived in the desert; the Pintubi, the Pitjantjatjara? He had come such a distance already — from a village in Poland, stateless, a fugitive from war, his family exiled in Siberia — to make himself in the wilderness. Had he ever thought that it was for himself that he had come? He had not died here, but the others ... Strehlow's agonising departure from life. Lasseter ... dying slowly of starvation, the ants devouring him; scribbling ... messages: to his wife, instructions, directions to the reef, his fear of the 'blacks' who had tried to help him. What must they have thought of the strange dying demented white man and his feverish scribbling and scrabbling to bury his words. They wouldn't have known about gold, the voracious hunger for it, the delusions. Leichhardt, the scholar, wandering in circles perhaps, seeking The Way, The Answer. She'd read his story, drawn to the mystery like others before her. A few bones, a scrap of leather ... lying somewhere unknown. Solitary deaths, solitary compulsions. And the savage outbreaks of slaughter — the massacres, the madness for the land that drove the Europeans to a frenzy. It seemed now to Zoe that the riverbed was moving, dark shapes rose and subsided in the deep shadow of the canyon. In the space she had entered without reckoning, she saw men on horseback, and crowding bodies heaving to escape, the upraised arms of men, women and children herded like beasts. Lasseter, tormented and desperate to be saved; the skull-visage of Leichhardt, stripped of flesh. The missionaries were there, the heavy bodies sweating and ill in grim determination to render God in their own shape; the wraiths, thin as a wisp of bitter smoke twisting up in a drunken despairing anger. All of this she saw in the moving mass of shadows; a Golgotha, a chasm of horror, created out of what she knew, what she had seen, what had been done. They called, strange sounds echoing back — a sharp scream, a sudden stillness — the ravine was crowded with them. How bizarre and unfitting this convergence was. How violent and unrelenting the engagement, once begun. They would never stop, she saw that. They would be lost if they did. They wanted everything — the land and its spirit and even then they would not be content. She hoped the Aranda, the Pitjantjatjara, whoever was left, understood that: that they were locked in an unending combat for the land. It had become irrelevant that it would not support those who wanted it in the way they expected. It was too old and fragile. Its age-old cycles of wind and rain and searing bleaching heat subsumed their efforts, and their endeavours were as nothing. She had seen the evidence.

Moving out of the shadows, the cattle climbed the steep path. Now she could see their horns catching the moonlight, hear the crack and rub of their hooves and bodies. Again — the sharp scream of a night creature capturing its quarry. She ran, Zoe Madden, her hair streaming in disarray, heedless of falling, her heart pumping in fear of being overtaken. Oh, I am mad, she thought, afraid of the darkness she had called up out of her own mind. In her fright, she could not bear to look back. That drumming, that stamping. She had read Zane Grey, she had watched John Wayne movies, she had read *Manshy* at school. She would be run down, trampled under the hooves. She fled down the track, the sinewy legs of a country woman flashing white in the moonlight spooking the wild steers.

Zoe slowed to a walk when she reached the safety of buildings, her shoes crunching on the gravel surface. In the shower she let the hot water pour over her, calming her breathing, flushing her mind of the images. Out of the pit of Europe she'd called them up, the dark discordances imposed on the seamless unity of a people and their land. She grasped the chain of consequence that followed the act of leaving the home place for another; the unhealed rupture; the gap, the silence, the distortions of history. For once she didn't care about the hot water supply; surely by morning it would be replenished.

Tom half-woke when she climbed into bed beside him.
    'Where have you been,' he mumbled.
    She huddled against him. 'I've been transgressing, out there. Did you hear that noise?'
    'Sounded like cattle. Go to sleep, Zoe, it's been a long day.'
    She eased the curtain back so she could see the moon declining behind the mountain. She listened to the regular pattern of Tom breathing, warming herself against the inert mass of his body. He was the fulcrum against which she turned and swung, the limit of the arc of her life since she had been a girl, as she was of his, probably. They had married so young — everybody did in that generation, after the war — it followed that balance and rhythm were essential to continuance. If they were twin pendulums, then their safe movement through the arc was critical, dependent

on the absence of shocks that would alter the measure between them. How extraordinary, she thought, to have lived so precariously for so long without knowing it. She watched the moonlight play on the mountain, changing its shape, until she slept.

At the Bottom of the River

It was, after all, the driest season in memory. They said there had always been stretches of water left before, deep pools, sufficient until the rains came. But this year the monsoons had failed and *The Oldest Riverbed in the World* was exposed. If there were secrets, they were uncovered.

Zoe had gone on alone. 'This might never happen again,' she told Tom. 'No one might ever see this again, for generations — for hundreds of years.'

He was dubious. 'It goes on for miles. Sand and stone — haven't you seen enough?'

'No.' She was definite. 'No I haven't.'

'Well, I've had enough. I'm going back.' He expected her to give up.

'I'll go on a bit further.'

He considered her. 'We'd better agree on a time.'

'A couple of hours,' she said. 'I'll see you in a couple of hours.' She slung the water flask over her shoulder. 'I'll be all right.' Go, she told herself. before something stops you.

She began walking in the fine white sand, waving to him over her shoulder. Walking lightly with an easy stride, her body poised. Choosing her path through the stones. Willing him not to come after her.

The Oldest, The Biggest, The Deepest ... They had come across the signs in unexpected places and doubted the veracity; smiled at the boldness of some of the claims. Sometimes it was the wry humour of the claim; a joke. Sometimes a kind of innocence; the optimism of small settlements that looked inward and saw only themselves reflected, believing the magnification. At others it was an opportunism, the shrewd instinct that traps the traveller in odd places. But the river — the river was something different.

Zoe had read the geological details on the ranger's information sheet. The Finke River. Ancient beyond comprehension. This was where the life of the region had been archived: the cataclysms of nature; the history of occupation; law, ceremony and ritual; tragedies and travesties ... Water concentrated life. Without it there was nothing. But even here there were long droughts that drove the cattlemen and the missionaries out. Life dwindled down, down, to the nucleus, perhaps; all knowledge concentrated in the survivors. Namatjira had walked here with his father, Arrernte men. In their own place. The alteration in the pattern of wind and rain — a momentary aberration in the scale of eons — and her being here, was a coincidence she could not ignore. She needed time and there was never enough.

She had expected to escape patterns on this journey — and routines; to be free of the need to comply. Instead, new patterns had formed, new routines. When had they begun to make a ritual out of it? Travelling from place to place, only staying for so long, having to move on. They were rushing ... Time was always against them: the change of seasons, the harvest, the market ... distance. These were the imperatives that drove them.

All her life she had fitted into the pattern. A mosaic, so tightly constructed that if one piece moved, the whole pattern was threatened. She longed to be random. Yes. That was it. To think and move at random. To proceed or draw back as she wished, impelled by nothing more than the need of the moment.

She passed people who were walking back to the car park, nodded to them, kept going. Until she *felt* she was alone she would not stop. Then, she told herself, I will sit down and rest.

In the stillness, as absolute as a held breath, Zoe chose her way through a jumble of fallen rocks; places where the force of the river had scoured the walls, cutting and shaping its passage. Seams and cracks traced the outline of vast slabs of rock in the process of dissolution, of falling. A falling which might be centuries long, or seconds. With each movement of her body she entered further into an unknown calculation in which time and the language of its measurement lost meaning.

Ahead of her, she saw the canyon walls rising on each side, converging. This was where the tourist parties turned back.

When she entered the narrow passage it was cold. The sun could not reach the depths. In the thin light the walls were blue-grey, veined with threads of minerals; the colour of viscera. The sand had the sharp smell of damp. She walked steadily, not hurrying, intent only on penetrating further. She reached out to touch the wall where it rose sheer and solid out of the riverbed. It was smooth against her

114

palm. She paused, resting her forehead against it. She would never be so close again.

In the distance the riverbed seemed to rise and widen. She could see the sunlight striking off the walls. It was a natural point to make for; the opening out, the sunlight. Now, in the cold narrow passage the walls were so high they seemed to have closed over her. There were no others here. No footprints. She felt a breathlessness, a consciousness of the unimaginable weight of stone bearing on her. She drew in the thin air, reluctant to exhale, as if, in its release, she might lose too much of herself. An alignment of the walls closed off the narrow shaft of sky. She fought an impulse of panic. Continued. Moved forward. Her passage soundless on the fine white sand. She touched the blue visceral walls, willing herself to know it as she went. To be unafraid of the shadow.

Out in the light, in the explosion of warmth and brilliance, Zoe stumbled over the stones. She was seeking a resting place; temporary haven. She wanted the sun to take away the chill in her bones and the feeling of ordeal. Ahead she could see a concavity at the base of the wall, a sun-warmed hollow. She climbed towards it, anticipating the pleasure of lying in warm scoured sand. She was exhausted. Here the sand smelled sweet. Above her, birds wheeled in the blue dome. She knew she would sleep, that the irresistible act of sleeping marked a point in the journey. She had surrendered to the place she was in, and she would trust it.

It was the tapping of the hammer on stone that woke her. The trickle of falling debris as the man worked his way across the rockface opposite. She watched him, secure and hidden in her sleeping place. He was on a narrow ledge, an extrusion which followed a fault line. There were shallow concavities along the seam, and in these the man would stop to gouge and work at the rock, prising off pieces which he placed in the bag slung over his shoulder. The ledge disappeared into the wall and she watched to see what the man would do when he reached that point. Spreadeagled there, his arms and legs outstretched against the wall, he looked ridiculously vulnerable. With painstaking care, he sought for handholds and footholds, working his way down to the riverbed.

Zoe watched him jump the last couple of metres, the weighted bag of stones falling forward. He regained his feet and stood, looking around him. With a flicker of excitement, she saw that he believed himself to be alone. He sat on the sand, leaning his back against the smooth half-buried stone in the riverbed. He took a small flask from his bag and sipped from it.

Motionless, her body now relaxed and rested, Zoe scrutinised the man. His head tipped back. Resting. He was not young, but not old either. Not a strong-looking man, yet he had managed the climb down the sheer part of the wall without difficulty. His skin was burned a reddish-brown. His hair — brownish, perhaps greying — was cut short and neat. She unfastened her own canteen and drank a little, keeping her eyes on the man. He had fallen asleep. Innocent and unaware that she was watching him.

She was in no hurry. Unexpected, the thought came to her that the man was hers. That his life — while he was unaware — rested with her. She remembered the guilty excitement, as a child, of tracking a small animal, a lizard pehaps. Trapping it. The moment when she would decide whether to extinguish it, or let it go; her curiosity with its struggle to escape. She had forgotten that feeling — of power.

She got to her feet, stepping with care down towards the man, careful not to disturb him. He was deeply asleep. She stood over him, noting the white skin of his eye-sockets, the fan of white lines at his temples. She saw the pulse beating in his throat, the rise and fall of his chest. His hands, resting on his stomach, were long and bony. The skin on the knuckles was scraped, the nails clipped short and clean; the hands of a man who did not work manually. His boots were those the European travellers wore. She sat a little way from him. Waiting.

When he came awake he stayed still. Looking around. He was startled when he saw her and sat up, brushing a hand over his head. 'Who are you?' She smiled at the foolishness of it. What answer did he expect to get? 'Where have you come from?' The English had an accent.

Zoe leaned forward, resting her arms on her knees. Amused at his discomfort. 'I've been here all the time. You looked like a little lizard spread out up there.' She gestured to the wall. 'What were you doing? Weren't you afraid the rock would give way?'

They looked at the wall. The narrow ledge was undercut. A deep crack ran above it. The whole section of wall was poised to fall.

'It is very interesting for me,' he said.

'Where are you from?'

'Hannover.'

'Oh. You are German. Germans have been coming here for many many years.'

He smiled. 'Yes, there are many German names here.'

'On the map, maybe. Did you find what you were looking for?'

'I am looking for fossils. I am a palaeontologist.'

'You must not take anything from here,' she said softly. 'Nothing. That is all finished now.'

His eyes flicked to the specimen bag. 'Are you ...?' His uncertainty was obvious. 'Are you from around here?'

He was properly awake now. What would it be like? She would have to decide — quickly.

'Close by.' She was pleased with the perfect ambiguity of it; at the beginning of what she was doing *now* she had come from *here*. How much could she get away with — that was the point. He was studying her: her dusty unironed shirt and skirt, her unevenly pigmented skin which could not take the sun. He could never be sure. She could easily complicate any rules of identification he might apply. She touched her wild tangle of red hair. 'My father was an Irishman.' She was mocking him. 'They are like the Germans — you find them everywhere ... Do you have permission to dig in the walls with your little hammer?' She lifted her foot and put it firmly on the leather satchel he'd dropped beside him, letting the implications expand to fill the silence.

'You were unlucky to meet me.' She paused. 'This is Arrernte country.' The silence wrapped her like the softest cloak. A feathered mantle that almost enabled her to fly. She was high ... high on it. The thrill of a dangerous game. 'Do you know Hermannsburg?'

'I have visited there. There are no German people there now.'

'Why did they come in the first place? Can you tell me that?' She had him hooked now, at least half-convinced. (He'd be thinking: red hair, freckled patchy skin. Mixed race, multi-lingual?) If only she had some real words. She would have to improvise. Confuse him. Black was not always black in Australia. Did he know that? Besides, she wanted to hear what he would say.'What is your opinion?' she asked, letting her skirt fall bunched and loose between her knees, aware of him looking at her. Deliberately, she provoked him, let him think *he* was the hunter ...'Why here? No one asked them to come.'

'Ah, yes — the Lutherans, of course. Very dedicated. I believe they would have come with a mission to convert the primitive black — ' He stopped.

'Difficult, isn't it? Especially for you. With your history.' She could see he was a little angry. He would get up and leave any minute. He seemed a nice man. Polite but uneasy. Unsure of what he had got into. But the confidence was still there. He wasn't worried. She could go a bit further ...

'Don't worry,' she said, 'We're used to it. We grew up on it. That's what makes this country so violent.' Her mouth shaped a half-smile. 'A bad conscience makes people nasty. Around here they used to shoot people like dogs. Ride them down and shoot them. Starve them ... Hunt them away from the waterholes ... Bloodthirsty. It didn't make any difference in the long run how they did it. Guns or religion. It ended up the same ... Nowadays it's the booze and disease ...'

She rested her head on her knees, hiding her face from him.

He was gentle. 'But things are different now ... Surely it is different now?'

'Nothing is different,' she said. 'Below the surface nothing is different.'

The sun had moved over. Where they sat was in deep shadow. The walls had turned the strange greyish-blue colour again. She remembered where she had seen it before — that colour. It was the cord. The purplish-grey membrane pulsing with blood. Exposed. Before the cut ... It was time to move.

'Are you a Christian?'

He shook his head. 'I am a scientist. Bones are my field. Very old bones.'

119

'They are mine too, in a way.' Relics ... Let him think she meant ancestors ... but she was thinking of the priest's altar stone, the relic it contained; the power of it. The awful weight of sacrifice — the child's dread of being responsible.

'My parents were Christians, Lutherans, in fact. My great-grandfather came to South Australia to escape persecution.'

'Ah ...' her breath was soft on the air. 'Is it difficult to be a German?'

He was standing. 'Please,' she said, staying him. 'Is it hard to bear? The reminders, the anniversaries ...'

He was brushing the sand from his clothes, his movements sharp and hurried. 'I am a scientist.'

She shook her head slightly, denying him. 'In here,' touching her diaphragm to steady herself, feeling the pulse pounding in her chest (*out of the past ... the old habit ... the words ... the power of them ... culpa, mea culpa*). She pursued him. 'How do you live with it? Your past.' She watched him, cruel in her detachment. 'Atonement,' she whispered. 'You see?'

'I am sorry,' he muttered, his accent thicker.

She stood to face him. 'You'd better go now.' She pointed down the riverbed, to the dark cleft between the walls.

'May I have my bag?'

She emptied the stones from it and handed it to him.

He shrugged. He would not look at her. She saw the gooseflesh on his arms. The riverbed was cold in the deep shadow of the walls.

The German slung the bag over his shoulder, quickening his pace as he walked away. Before he got too far she reached down and selected a rock from those he'd collected, and took aim. It landed beside him. He began to hurry. She selected another, releasing it with a strong overarm throw that sent it hurtling. It caught him on the shoulder. He stumbled and began to half run, scrambling over the stones. The last rock she aimed at the wall so it would ricochet into the passage, absolving her of where it may fall. In the dead silence the impact was an avalanche of sound.

She went back to the small clearing where they had talked, scuffing the sand with her feet. The chill was in her bones again. She began to move — the steps of a dance. It was ancient. She needed the sway and rhythm of it; to get back. Her grandmother had taught her. Sometimes her mother would join them, and her sisters. Swaying and bending, they would drone the words, not knowing where they came from, just knowing them, secure and close in their circle. It was from the old country, a women's dance. The simple movements warmed and soothed her body.

Zoe entered the van quietly. It was hot and airless. He had fallen asleep waiting for her, the perspiration pooling on his bare chest and stomach. She touched him lightly and he woke with a start, tensing in a protective reflex action. 'I wouldn't hurt you,' she said. He was looking at her and she stared back. Waiting for him to speak.

'You look exhausted. How far did you go?'

She hesitated. 'A long way.'

'Was it worth the effort?'

His eyelids were dark, she noticed, a strange attractive tinge. Delicately, she rested a finger on the skin. In the muted light inside the van he looked foreign, the beard he was growing changed him.

'Where do you come from?' She was half-serious.

'I don't know,' he said. 'No one ever told me.'

She lay on the bed beside him, languor overtaking her.

'Marooned with a stranger,' she said, turning away. 'So far from home.'

The Plateau

There was an undercurrent of doubt in their decision to take the old man's advice and go to Kings Canyon. Wherever they went next, there were no short cuts, few possibilities. Time was beginning to press on Tom. He thought more about the orchard. They were spending capital, next year's living if the market went bad again.

They passed the unsealed road turning off the Stuart Highway near Henbury and continued on towards Erldunda. The truck had stood up well but it needed an oil change; the tyres were showing wear and Tom wanted to attend to it before they went further inland. On the way through Alice Springs, they had stopped to stock up on food.

'Don't you want a newspaper?' Tom had asked Zoe.

'No. I want to get going.'

'That's not like you.'

She had put the headphones on — Schumann's piano cycle (her mother had played it late at night when everyone was in bed). The sonatas were familiar, a connection which held no threats or surprises; a sound of ease. Once again they were adrift on the vastness, and loneliness had crept on them. They stopped for a mid-morning coffee at a bleak truck bay, the piercing cold wind gusting around them. Without delaying they resumed driving.

Tom had talked to the old man on their last night at Glen Helen. They'd met him before, at Broome, when they'd just arrived at their first caravan park. Overwhelmed by the crowd of travellers and unsure of what they were doing, they'd been tempted to stay put, drifting in the pleasant limbo of indecision. The old man had strolled past one evening and stayed talking. He was in his seventies and had been everywhere and done everything: a cattleman, a crocodile shooter, a pearler, a prospector, a surveyor. He had spent part of the war as a coastwatcher, island hopping in an outrigger canoe. He had been married to a Yolngu woman — so he said.

At Glen Helen, the old man was almost taciturn. 'What you've seen is nothing,' he told them over a drink. 'There are a hundred gorges in these ranges the tourists will never get to see.'

'Why?' Zoe asked.

'Too hard to get in. Too precious ...'

'Have you been there?'

He was evasive. 'I'm past that now. Where are you heading for?'

Tom was casual. 'We might poke around here for a few more days, then head south to Uluru. We have to think about heading west.'

'Go to Kings Canyon,' the old man said, draining his glass. 'Go there first.'

Zoe had left them talking, sensing the old man's relief when she excused herself.

'What did you talk about?' she'd asked Tom when he came back to the van.

'Nothing much.' Tom didn't tell Zoe that the old man had urged him to get going. 'Mark my words,' he'd said. 'You want to get your woman out of here. There's too much going on. Head out to Kings Canyon, that's the place to go. It's quiet out there.'

His battered Willys jeep was gone when they got up next morning.

Zoe had remarked on it: 'He only got here last night.'

Luritja Road turned off the sealed road to Yulara. In the late afternoon the narrow earth road disappeared between lines of thick verge growth. There were signs of old mud slides, deep wheel ruts. There had been rain recently.

Tom read the notation on the map: *Roads shown as earth-formed have gravel sections which can become quickly affected by rain and remain impassable for varying periods ...* They had not told anyone where they were going. Who was there to tell? He could have mentioned it at Erldunda, but he hadn't — it would have seemed a bit overanxious.

While Zoe boiled the kettle for tea and made sandwiches, Tom walked along the track. It looked all right. Having chosen to go via Erldunda, this was the only way to reach Kings Canyon. The old man had been so insistent. There was also something different about the landscape — the soft piled earth on the verges, the vegetation, the stands of desert oak — something open which appealed to him; less contrived and controlled than the main tourist pathway. If there were a few rough patches it would give him something to concentrate on; he had begun to tire of the monotonous driving on the highway through country that was inaccessible, yielding nothing.

Now that he had made his decision they would have to hurry. There was seventy-odd kilometres of dirt track before they connected with the road into Kings Canyon, and that was not surfaced either. There were no points in between where they could break the journey. While Zoe scrambled cups and food into cupboards. Tom walked around the truck checking that everything was secured. There would be no turning back. The truck with its top-heavy campervan was not designed for rough roads.

In the fading light, the desert oaks were in relief, elegant and delicate tracings against the skyline. The soft verges rose on either side, enclosing the vehicle, flattening, falling away temporarily to bare plains through which the track cut a straight line over eroded and uneven stone. Clouds of white birds bloomed on bare trees, rose and fell again as they passed. They were impelled by the road — the drifts of loose sand, the short sections of savage corrugations — to keep going without slackening speed. In the rushing compulsion, the swift loom and loss of the desert oaks against the changing sky colours, their passage had the force of a dream: a claustrophobic and inescapable interval after which there would be a difference, a change, an arrival of some kind.

Darkness was closing on them when the tunnel of light from their headlamps showed the road suddenly widening onto a hard gravel surface. They had reached a crossroad. Tom eased the truck to a halt on the edge of the intersection. Outside the warm closed interior of the cab, the black chill of the desert night enveloped them. They crouched in the pool of light, spreading the map on the ground.

'There's only one road and this must be it. We go west.'

'What if it's a surveyor's road?' Zoe was nervous.

'No, this carries a bit of traffic. It's been recently graded. It's all right,' he reassured her. 'Look at the map. There is nothing else. Nothing.'

It was true. One road, ending at Kings Canyon, none of the spidery lines that indicated tracks to cattle stations or Aboriginal communities. No indicators of points of interest, no fuel stops. 'We are here,' Tom showed Zoe, pointing to the intersection. 'We turn left and drive until we reach Kings Canyon, or — we turn around and go back the way we came.'

Tom drove steadily, alert and focused, wary of driving into the night without any sense of the country they were passing through. Without reference points it seemed that the road existed only within the range of the headlights, disappearing behind, creating itself in front of him. For all he knew, it was a pathway into nothing. When he had decided to go on he had committed them to it. He thought now of the way in which small decisions are made which could turn out to be vital. Like deciding not to stay at Erldunda for the night and waste the afternoon doing nothing, to deviate from their original plan to stay on main roads; not telling anyone where they were going. He had noted on the map the emptiness of the area they were heading into: desert on one side, mountains on the other; country which was hard and barren and uninhabited. The emptiness fascinated him and it filled him with dread. He began an inventory of his resources: what he was capable of, what he could do, how he would manage situations. He was not usually a risk-taker; that way, he stayed out of trouble. But he had gone against his habits — the way he did things. The old man had influenced him, had made it seem almost ... urgent; a place he must see. Where he would normally be detached, content to let the journey unfold, now he was expectant, impatient. *That* was why he had pushed on. He glanced over at Zoe. She was asleep. Good. It meant he was free to drive, to let his thoughts wander. Her restlessness distracted him.

Sometimes Tom longed to be home with a fierceness that startled him. Home in his own place, where he was in control, where he knew what he was doing. Where the scale of things was within the boundaries of what he could deal with. It was tiring him, this long drawn out passage over immeasurable distances. He could see the advantage of staying in one place, of limiting one's horizon to what was manageable. He tried to imagine what it would be like to go with the country, not to work it or change it but to ... trust oneself to it ... completely. He thought of what he had seen: the vast floodplains of rivers, the eroded nub of mountains, the savagery of gibber plains, the evidence of the relentless power of nature to sweep away, in an instant, the trivial bulwarks of man. He caught a sense, briefly, of what it must be like to have the knowledge and ability to go with it like that; to be part of it; the exhilaration a man could feel.

It was very different for him. He cared about his land — hill, stone, river and soil — but he was in constant tension with it. He had to make it produce for him, otherwise he would be unable to keep it. That was the problem: how was he going to hold on to it? Some of his neighbours had ripped out their fruit trees and planted pines on the slopes. He hated pine plantations. The cold dark alleys of sour ground, the incessant sighing of the wind high in the trees, the dead quietness on the carpet of pine needles. Sixty kilometres down the road from his land, they mined the sand and produced titanium. There'd been controversy over the waste turning the adjacent land radioactive. It was where he'd spent his summers as a child, camping in the groves of peppermint trees, swimming and fishing in the estuary. A hundred kilometres the other way, they mined tantalum and lithium. Rare earths ... He suspected that there were valuable deposits on his land. His grandfather hadn't been too wrong when he'd pegged the valley. There mightn't have been much gold but there were other minerals — more valuable than gold. That's why he hated anyone poking around. Even Jeremy, his own son, who had grown up on the place. Jeremy would mine it, or sell it tomorrow; he'd be making deals with mining companies if he knew there was tantalum or lithium there. I should be there now, Tom thought, keeping a watch on things. He had let the mining rights go, but as soon as he got home he'd look into it. He imagined the nightmare of discovering someone else had pegged the land in his absence. He toyed with the idea of asking Jeremy to check, then decided against it. Better to keep it to himself.

Recently he'd had a recurring dream. The steep hills on the north side were pouring soil. It was so clear: the fine chocolate topsoil pouring like liquid down the slopes, leaving black glistening granite uncovered. In the dream he and his grandfather were working desperately to stem the flow; straining to roll boulders into its path, chopping at trees, but it was unstoppable, pouring over them, choking them. It was after he'd had that dream that he woke up feeling tired, his head cloudy, his limbs heavy and sluggish.

Tom saw with relief that the road surface ahead was sealed.

The sound of the motor changed and woke Zoe. 'Are we there?' she asked.

'No, about halfway. I don't think we're going to make it

tonight.' The road was built on a high bed. Deep cuttings each side made it dangerous even to attempt to pull onto the verge. Zoe chattered, keeping him awake, but the need to sleep was insistent. It had become an ordeal.

Tom saw what looked like a turn-off coming up. It was the only break in the road he had seen. They had passed no other vehicles since the afternoon but he was not prepared to park on the road. He took the chance, slowing down, bumping off the bitumen onto the track. It looked hard enough, an old gravel pit for the road-making most likely. The track twisted and turned, taking them deeper into the bush.

'I don't like this,' Zoe said. 'We're going too far in.'

'We'll have to make the best of it.' He was exhausted. 'It will have to do.' In a small clearing he turned the truck in a half-arc and switched off the motor.

They climbed out of the truck, stiff from the long day's travel. The loss of heat from the cab made them shiver instantly.

Tom lit the gas lamp and, while Zoe began to look for tins to open, he collected what wood he could find in the truck headlights.

'Don't worry about a fire,' Zoe called to him. 'We'll eat and then go to bed.'

'We'll get too cold and I don't want to leave the lights on too long.' There was no pretense that they were comfortable. Outside the field of light the darkness was impenetrable.

The dry wood blazed quickly and they sat close to it while the food heated. Tom walked the perimeter, disappearing briefly into the darkness.

'Tom,' Zoe called sharply. 'Where are you?'

'It's all right,' he called back. He reappeared dragging a branch.

They were uneasy, not attempting to hide it. He had stumbled over cans and bottles. There'd been drinking parties here. Not tourists, they didn't stay long enough to leave rubbish like that. Maybe the road gang had camped here, but it didn't look like it — they usually cleaned up before they left. There was a bad feeling to the place.

They ate quickly, letting the fire burn down. Tom checked the truck, taking items from the glove box and their travel bags into the van before he locked it. They closed themselves in the small space, latching the van door. Zoe said nothing as Tom slipped a screwdriver through the catch.

Sometime during the night they were woken by sounds outside. They lay still. Listening.

'Dingoes,' Tom said.

The morning was grey, with heavy cloud closing out the sun. In daylight the place was ugly and desolate. Around the van were dog tracks.

They left immediately, winding their way through bracken following the twisting track.

'We're on a floodplain,' Tom said. 'We'd be in trouble if we were caught here.'

When they regained the road, their spirits lifted.

'They were dingo tracks weren't they?'

'Looking for food,' Tom said.

Zoe shivered. 'I don't want to think of them prowling around us.'

Tom didn't mention the campsites he'd seen, or the shotgun shell cases strewn in the bushes. It was over now. But he thought how much they took on trust. How little they knew — about what they were doing. They made assumptions as they went, ignorant of the possibilities.

Kings Creek camping ground was less than thirty kilometres further along the sealed road from their night camp. They took their time cooking breakfast, sitting outside in the weak sunlight watching the activity. Another thunderstorm seemed to be building. Tom was keyed up. Everyone was on the move: packing up tents, closing up caravans ready to go. He and Zoe were out of kilter with the general movement. He had the niggling feeling, again, that his judgement was off. He was annoyed with himself for being susceptible to what others were doing. Later, he was taciturn in the exchange with the fuel attendant, avoiding conversation.

While Tom was fuelling up, Zoe went into the shop and bought mineral water and snacks. She read the signs posted up for tourists, printed in Japanese and German as well as English. Warnings: *Consider your health and fitness for the walk. Do not walk in the hottest part of the day.* There were instructions on how to treat dehydration and heart failure, how to contact the ranger in emergencies. She picked up the walking map and went out to wait for Tom.

The sealed road led them to the entrance to the canyon. In the small car park there were two vehicles. While they gathered their bags, a light pack each, two Japanese men appeared and got into one of the vehicles.

Zoe waved to them. 'We should have asked them about the climb. We met them at Tennant Creek. Remember?'

'We're not on our own anyway,' Tom said, indicating the other car.

The short walk through a narrow canyon led them to a sudden confrontation with the wall they would have to climb to reach the rim of the canyon. It was a precipitous path hacked out of the stone.

'My God,' Zoe said. 'I can't climb that.'

Tom sighed in exasperation. Nothing had gone quite right since they had changed their plan to come here. They were getting tired, that was part of it; but in other ways their tolerance was being depleted. They were at their furthest point from home. There was no quick and easy way out of it. 'What are you going to do?' He waited for her, suppressing his annoyance.

'It's so high, it's a cliff. I'd get vertigo.'

'I'm going to do it. Do you want to wait here?'

'No!'

He didn't blame her. It was lonely. The country was hard and unappealing. There was no pretense in the approach to the place that it was anything other than an endurance test. He wandered over to the information signs. *Stop and check your fitness for this walk ... six kilometres around the top of the canyon before descending to the car park. Take robust footwear, drinking water and a hat. In the event of an emergency contact the ranger.* The instructions were detailed.

They came to a halt at a memorial plaque for someone who had died attempting the walk.

Why do it? Tom thought. What pushed sensible mature people to leave a comfortable life and spend thousands of dollars of their life savings to take risks in the middle of nowhere? Everywhere they had been it was the same. Everyone he talked to ... *have you been here — have you been there*. Measuring. Comparing. They drove themselves to keep going. They came from all over the country and they were all doing the same thing. They started out like he and Zoe had probably, thinking it was easy — *See The Country* — and then, somehow, they got caught up in it. Trying to prove something. Christ knows what. If they were honest, half of them would admit they'd had enough, were dog-tired, or fed up with each other. But Tom knew, in his heart, what it was. They had to prove they weren't frightened of it, that they could do it, and, for the moment, he was one of them: stubborn people who would not give up. If they did, they had to go back to where they lived and admit they'd failed. If they didn't beat the country, it would beat them.

But he *had* seen defeat on this journey and he had wondered about it. Numerous defeats, in many shapes and forms: the landscape flayed and scraped bare, and then left ... like a skin nailed to a wall to dry, the flesh and guts cut away. He had watched, as a boy, his grandfather and father skinning kangaroos and possums; knew intimately the look and feel of the parchment skin, the blue tracery of dry veins; a last reminder of the warm body that had filled it. The country, in places, had made him think of that. The ruins of settlement, the mines — gold, tin, asbestos, wolfram, uranium — abandoned. The shabby little towns which seemed to be just hanging on, but each with its video store and lotto agency; the clusters of black people hanging around. Waiting, as if they knew it was inevitable that in the end everyone else would give up and go away, defeated. Outside the cities, nothing seemed to last. The efforts of men like his grandfather and himself, to reshape the landscape and hold the change in a permanent form, had no certainty. They could alter it, but in some way he could not fathom, it was impossible to ... to trust it. The image of the dream returned: the soil flowing down into the river. And the river was sick. He'd told no one. The sprays kept the fruit unblemished — he used them like everyone else, but he wasn't happy about it. In the run-off channels, the water weed was rotten and dead ... He could remember when the streams were crystal clear and he used to drink from them. Mistakes had been made — from the beginning. They had been too greedy, too impatient. Some kind of alliance with the land had not been made and now it was going wrong. A pulse began to beat in his temple. A headache was threatening to start, and he turned abruptly, walking back to Zoe.

'Well? If we're going to do it we'd better make a move, before it gets too late.'

'I'm ready,' she said.

They climbed slowly. Tom close behind Zoe, encouraging her, telling her where to put her hands, her feet, persuading her — not to look down, or up, to look only at the wall. In the combined effort, the bodily closeness, they moved together, crabbing their way up the rockface.

'Will it ever end?' Zoe gasped.

'Yes, keep going. We can't stop now.'

They rested. Zoe had crawled away from the rim, refusing to look behind her. She sat now on the sheet rock, her back against the stone. Tom had gone close to the edge, looking out at the immense reach of folding ranges and distant mesas, the endless bare plains; an emptiness that caught at his throat. He swallowed. He could feel the blood pounding in his temples. A light wind curled around him, cooling his sweating body. Clouds hid the sun, but the heat was only temporarily suspended. The dry exhilarating air parched his lips and throat.

They sat, side by side, their faces flushed with exertion.

'We made it,' Zoe said. She opened a bottle of water and filled two beakers, unwrapped a chocolate, giving him half.

'Yes, we made it.' He mopped his face with his hand-kerchief, not sure what was happening to him. He realised that Zoe was peering at him, her face taut with fright.

'Are you all right?'

'Yes, yes,' he waved her away. 'I'm all right.' His chest felt heavy and tight. 'I've just overdone it a bit.'

Zoe had removed his hat and was fanning him. She took his handkerchief and doused it with water, wiping his face. He tried smiling at her, trying to reassure her, but his face felt stiff.

'Just stay still.' She sat beside him, watching him. 'We forget we are getting old.'

'I'm not old,' he said. 'I'm just tired.' He looked at her. Zoe. She had lost weight since they started. She looked ... weathered. The bones in her face showing through, sharper. It suited her. She looked a little comical in the baggy shorts and old loose shirt buttoned to the wrist, her hat pulled down to shade her face. Wisps of hair sticking out. The brown eyes and the red hair ... He'd known her all his life and he could not remember the last time he had really looked at her. She had always been there, but somehow at arm's length.

There had been four of them — until Dolly died. But it was three he remembered. Three sisters, with gold and red and auburn hair. He closed his eyes and he could see and smell them: drying their hair in the sun, the fragrance of it, the warm sweetness of skin touched with sweat, the curve of their white arms as they lifted their hair and spread it to dry. He had ached for them, had wanted to bury himself in their soft flesh and they had teased him, rolling him in the lush summer grass, pinning him down, Sophie and Clare, knowing what they were doing to him, and Zoe, the youngest, less knowing and less exciting to him than her older sisters. He had wanted the whole family: the noise and clutter, the intensity; the arguing and joking. Loose, his mother had said, when he told her he was visiting the Maddens. Publicans and priests; and the women! The talk and the carrying on ... Loose. He had

135

*never seen his mother so distraught. He had married Zoe to be
part of it; to get away from the bitter silence in which he lived. He
could never tell Zoe that. But there was something ... a shock of
recognition.*

'I did have a place when I was a boy,' he said, not looking at
her as he spoke. 'An imaginary place — like this. A high
plateau — where no one could get at me. I could look out
and see anything coming, any movement. No one knew I
was there, and no one knew — except me — how to get up
there.'

'Were you alone?'

'Yes. That was the point of it. I wanted to be on my own ...'

'I think it would be terrifying. A place like this ... Why?'

He could feel the tightness in his chest, gripping him,
refusing to break.

'Because ... I suppose I couldn't handle the way things
were.' He stopped. *He didn't want to do this. He had kept it to
himself all these years. It went against the grain, but tension and
anger had been building in him for some reason, and worry —
being away for so long.*

Zoe waited.

He took a cautious, shallow breath. 'No one ever talked. Oh, now
and then there would be arguments. My mother would cry, the Old
Man would go down to the forge and my father ... would
disappear somewhere.'

'What was wrong, Tom?' She spoke quietly, drawing
herself in against what she might hear. It seemed imperative
to keep him talking, to ease his distress. But why here? she
was also thinking. Why this frightening place — where they were
cut off — where she was useless without him. Why now?

'It was the Old Man.' Tom sipped from the beaker of water. 'He
owned everything, you see, and he ... he despised my father

and mother. He used to say: *You'll never get anything of mine. He never gave my father any money — never paid him a wage, so he had to ask for everything.'*

'Why didn't your father leave?'

'The Depression, I don't know. No money. Nowhere to go. No one had anything. We used to have men coming to the farm, begging for a feed. When the war started my father joined up. It was a way out I suppose.'

Yes. A way out for his father, but he'd left his son to it. The Old Man had worked Tom harder. Before school and after school. Telling him: You've got to look after it. It'll be yours, one day, but you'll have to battle for it ...

'I thought it would be different when my father came back, you know ... the Returning Hero.' He stopped. 'Sorry about this.' He took a cautious breath. 'I'll be all right in a minute.' *What a mess! If something happened up here Zoe would have to get help, find the First Aid box and send up a flare for the ranger. It was humiliating. The bloody country got you in the end. Brought you down when you least expected it ... It didn't let you get away with anything.*

Tom made a move to get up and Zoe pressed him back. 'Don't move yet. We'll just sit here for a while. What happened when your father came back?'

'He was sick.'

Tom had seen him once. Crouched in the corner of the bedroom. His mother bending over him. She had looked up and seen Tom in the doorway and had come over and closed the door, shutting him out. He had gone to his room and escaped to the ... to the place. He had hated his father for being weak.

'He couldn't get over the war. He'd tried to escape a couple of times in Germany and they'd put him in solitary confinement. Old Geoff Lang told me that just a few years ago.'

It had been the first time he'd been told something. The only thing he knew which gave his father some personality. He'd wanted to ask questions but pride, or shame that he knew nothing, had stopped him.

'They were all captured in Crete. Those that weren't killed. Hardly a man left in the town ... all from the same division. The Old Man sent me away to college for a couple of years. I thought things would get better. Anyway — my father went up the hill one day, after rabbits, and ... shot himself.'

'Oh, God!' Zoe had known there was something ... But not that.

He had said it. It was out. 'I could have done something. I let it happen.'

He felt Zoe take his hand and he allowed it.

'No,' she said. 'Don't say that.'

But he wanted no comfort. There was no comfort. He had let it happen. He'd been angry with his father for leaving him. For not standing up to the Old Man. He was still angry, after all this time. So, he'd turned his back on his father. Gone with the Old Man.

'No one said a word. We just buried him. We said it was an accident. It happens.'

'I remember. Everyone saying it was sad, after surviving the war.'

No one had known the Drewes well, and there had been others with trouble in a small stricken community which had lost too many husbands and sons. Zoe had been away at university. When she'd come home on summer vacation, it was almost forgotten. Later, after marrying Tom, when she had entered the big white-shuttered house on the hillside surrounded by almond trees, she had been shocked to find the interior cold and lifeless, bereft of the presence of the people who had lived there. The bleakness had driven her to open windows, and hang her paintings, and surround herself with clutter. Tom had been generous in allowing her to take over and fill the place with her family and friends, and she saw now why he had done it: it was a remedy. And herself? Had she also been a part of that? An attempt to fill the emptiness? She sighed. 'It's all so long ago, we were so innocent. We thought the world couldn't touch us.' She spoke of herself, and for a moment she drew away, was detached from him — if she had not gone home that summer, if she had gone away to Europe like the others had. She turned her mind from it, from the awful danger of seeing too clearly. 'It hardly matters now,' she said aloud.

They sat together, their bodies touching at hip and shoulder, bound by habit and dependence, keeping their secrets.

'We'd better get going,' Tom said, 'we've got six kilometres to walk.'

'Do you feel all right?' Zoe frowned with concern.

'I'm fine.' He was brusque, making it clear that it was the end of it.

They stood up, stretching stiff leg muscles, adjusting their backpacks and hats, covering up again. Single file they entered the time-warp of sandstone domes rimmed with darker bands of strata. Tom went first, choosing the path. High up on the plateau, winding between the strange rock formations weathered to their nucleus, he had instants of memory, aftershocks which he didn't want to explore. He didn't want to know what else might be hidden in his memory. Already he was regretting what had happened. He had let Zoe in and he wondered what she would do with the knowledge. She had said — *it hardly matters now* — but he felt vulnerable all the same. Only in silence was he sure of his strength.

Tom had come to know what his mother had meant when she'd said that the Maddens were *loose:* they talked too much, a wild unpredictable tendency to dissent. They didn't seem to care what people thought about them.

'Ah, here is the *envoy*. Our messenger from the other side,' Athol Madden used to say when Tom entered their kitchen, sheepish but persistent. And they would laugh, an insider's laugh, a joke on him of some kind. He had never known when they were laughing at him. He had thought it was because he was not Catholic, not one of them, forever outside the mysterious union of their Faith. He knew the father had not trusted him — and was right in that. Tom *had* been a hunter — a predator — after his daughters. But it was more than that. It had hurt him, when he was young, he had wanted to be taken in; to be one of them. Out of bravado, he had asked Athol Madden if he could borrow the slim volume of McAuley's poems. He read 'Envoi' and puzzled over it: *There the blue-green gums are a fringe of remote disorder ... And there in the soil, in the season, in the shifting airs, Comes the faint sterility that disheartens and derides ... The people are hard-eyed, kindly, with nothing inside them ... independent but you could not call them free.* It had added to his uneasiness. He decided it was envy over the land, the wealth it implied. But he couldn't be blamed for that. *He* hadn't taken it from anyone. At some time, in the past, the valley had probably belonged to a tribe, been used by them, and someone, maybe his grandfather, had driven them off. They had gone anyway. Vanished. He had done no harm to anyone. It was different out here. He had seen for himself that another people had always been here and he could understand the pain of being driven off. He would feel the same. But he knew it was something to do with the land. Was that what Athol Madden had meant? That Tom was one of the *Takers*?

But wasn't everyone? Or had Athol just been playing with words as he often did, robbing another man's meaning to suit himself. Tom had never felt comfortable with him: the sharp wit and the mocking sarcasm about the English. He had felt the antagonism behind the wit. It was a bitter joke.

It had been a shock when he had gone through his grandfather's few personal possessions after he died. The document, a contract of employment, made out in the name of Tomas Dubrovic. Polish. A seaman — aged sixteen — from Gdansk. Signed on as an ordinary seaman, a merchant ship out of Gloucestor, USA — in 1890. He had told Tom once, in a rare moment of confidence, that he had jumped ship in Australia and walked to the goldfields. There had been more, but Tom had been impatient, a boy eager to get away. Tom had unfolded the other scraps of paper in the mildewed leather satchel the Old Man had kept in his wardrobe: a mining licence issued at Cue in 1894 in the name of Thomas Drewe. Letters, from London, barely decipherable, dated 1885! There was nothing else. Was the Old Man Drewe or Dubrovic — or both?

Wrapped in canvas, at the bottom of the satchel, was a heavy package. He could smell the gun oil. He had undone it carefully — an old handgun. Gingerly he checked the chambers. It was unloaded. He examined the mechanism, easing the hammer back. A single action revolver. A Webley. British. Tom had held the cold steel in his lap, felt the weight of it. It was an antique, but in perfect working order. The Old Man had looked after it. Carved into the butt were the initials *TD*. Who had it belonged to? He had rewrapped it carefully and put it back in the satchel. He would never know what had been done with it.

Tom had sat by the window of his house watching the mist rising up from the river. It would be typical of the Old Man to make fools of them ... let them think they were English farmers, the real thing, with a background. Secretive, hard old bastard. Who was *he* now? He had been Tom Drewe all his life, his name a thread connecting him to an unknown history; a mysterious counterweight holding him securely in place. Now he didn't even know if the land was his ... He was sure of nothing. He had stirred finally. Taken the contract, lit a corner and watched it turn black and curl into ash in the fireplace. Then he had searched the room meticulously. There was no will, nothing else with the name Dubrovic on it. He had replaced the other papers in the satchel and locked it in the desk drawer, removing the key.

He had sat for awhile in the armchair near the window, letting memory bring the Old Man back one last time. The tall, gaunt figure, lost in the heavy overcoat he wore in the winter. He was standing amongst the trees leaning on the staff he used on the slopes, out there to decide if there would be a frost, if the berries needed covering. Whoever he was, his grandson had loved him. He had been the unmoving centre. And now — he was gone.

When the European refugees — displaced persons they had called them — had arrived in the town in the fifties, silent and grim, the Old Man had had no sympathy. He'd refused to employ them because they spoke no English. *Peasants*, he'd called them. *Polacks*. After his death Tom had hired them, the last orchard in the district to employ the women as fruitpickers. He had been impatient with their few words of English, and hated their foreignness; hated the thought that he could have any connection with them. There was something tough and knowing in their eyes that made him nervous and arrogant. In time, their children had grown up and married into the community. Except for the names, you couldn't tell the difference now.

Tom and Zoe edged around an outcrop of rock and startled a couple deep in an embrace. They hurried past with averted eyes, hearing the laughter behind them.

'They're a long way from home,' Zoe said. With her ear for languages she had picked up the Italian. 'I suppose this is just another spectacle. I wonder if they have any sense of how extraordinary this place is.'

'Visitors, like us.' Tom said. 'We're only visitors. We have no more connection with this place than they do.' But he resented it all the same, the ability of strangers to come here and be casual about it. He felt the urge to go back and say something, make some kind of claim. He felt possessive — protective. It made no sense to feel that way, but he did; the more he thought about it, the more complicated it became. He had accustomed himself to the loneliness of uncertain connections.

They had reached the halfway mark. After a pause for breath, they began the steep descent down a series of stair-cases built on the canyon wall to a bridge crossing the chasm. Far below, at a depth which made it remote and fantastic, was an oasis. They could see the glint of water, the fronds of palm trees. Zoe clung to the railing enclosing the staircase. Peering, fearing the onset of vertigo. 'I wish we could get down there.'

Tom studied the wall and the narrow path they would have to climb down, turning to look at the bridge over the divide. 'It's too far.'

'It's always the way, isn't it,' Zoe said. 'Places we can't reach.'

143

They walked slowly, choosing their path along the edge of the canyon wall. Here, nature had been violent, cleaving the surface to a frightening depth. Hacking at the strata of the walls, exposing the hard core, leaving strange and grotesque extrusions hanging in space. And yet, at the heart of it, the innermost part, was the trickle of water and the softening growth of plant life; the slaked force transformed into the delicate pulse of renewal. Exhausted, they paused to rest. Tom climbed out onto a projection of rock to gaze back along the length of the canyon and down, down to the oasis.

'Come back! Come back,' Zoe cried out, covering her eyes, unable to look until he stood beside her. 'It's so dangerous,' she said.

He smiled at her, suddenly boyish and light. 'I've been here before, remember.' He touched her shoulder briefly. 'I'll stay away from the edge.' *He'd remembered the eagle. Soaring. The rush of wind. If he ever met the old man from Broome again he'd thank him for directing him here. But he didn't expect to. He had the feeling they'd moved out of the old man's territory. And he didn't even know his name.*

In the extremes of weariness they walked the last metres. It had become a matter of placing one foot after another in a safe position. They moved aside to let a group go through. It was the French family from Alice Springs. The woman brushed past, energetic and agile, the boy and girl scrambling after her, the man casual, nodding. The family was dressed alike in elegant climbing gear.

'How do they do it?' Zoe said.

'Do what?'

'Make you feel invisible.'

'If we were black they'd notice us.'

'*Indigenes*,' Zoe said. 'My great-grandfather was French —

on my mother's side.'

'Mine was ... European. I know that much.'

'We're nonentities,' she replied. 'Leftovers. No distinguishing features remain.'

They slept late, waking to a clear sunny day and a sense of aftermath. There was no point in staying on. They were beginning the journey home. They studied the map over a last cup of coffee. To the west, for thousands of kilometres, there was nothing but desert; no roads, no direct way through. It was the nature of the country; the line of progress infinitely drawn out.

Before they left they drove to the end of the road at Zoe's insistence. Then they stopped and walked, taking in the sun, the noise of birds, the hard impervious ground.

'Well, that's it,' she said. 'We'll never be here again.'

They settled themselves for travelling. Zoe tied her hair in a scarf and wound the window down, searched in her bag and found a packet of toffees.

'Like one?' she asked Tom, unwrapping it for him.

'Thanks,' he said, taking it from her outstretched hand.

Tomas Dubrovic

He left at night, making for Sandstone, avoiding the coach track to Day Dawn. He would work his way down to Coolgardie; once there he would decide where to go. The country could not be worse than he'd experienced coming down from the Kimberley. There had been a bit of rain, and there would be some water on the way down. The sooner he was away, the better. He knew too many up and down the tracks. And too many knew him: the Big Pole they called him.

In the full moonlight it was easygoing through the scrub. Near dawn he camped by a clump of saltbush, tethering the horse short so he wouldn't have to waste time finding him later. He drank from the canvas waterbag and poured water into an old dolly pan for the horse. They got cunning, these old nags; the horse didn't waste a drop. Before rolling into his swag, he ate a piece of cold damper and then slept. He woke at first light. Not bothering about breakfast, he began walking in the morning chill. Later, when it warmed up, he would rest and eat.

He'd come on the Englishman's camp well out from the main

diggings and had watched him, unseen, from a ridge. The man was ill. Around midday he had fallen and the Pole had walked down and dragged him into the tent out of the sun. The Englishman was delirious with fever. The Pole got him a drink from the barrel of water and swabbed his face with a wet cloth. He'd heard on the way down that they were dying like flies around Cue. Typhoid. He'd struck a few heading back north to the Yilgarn.

He sat in the tent through the afternoon, occasionally dribbling water into the Englishman's mouth, listening to his babbling. Around sunset he seemed better; his mind had cleared and he asked the Pole for his lettercase. In a weak scrawl he wrote: To Hannah Purton, Apothecary's daughter, and signed his name. He died soon after.

The Pole cooked himself a meal from the meagre supplies in the camp. He had gone three days without eating, and drunk the last mouthful of his water that morning. By candlelight he looked through the contents of the leather lettercase. Letters from England — the Englishman's family — the Apothecary's daughter. A passport, an English twenty pound note, a notebook with scribbled entries of moneys spent. A miner's right issued in Cue. He examined each item carefully. The letters were old, creased and faded, the last written in 1885, addressed to Fremantle. Ten years ago. The Pole was unmoved. He had seen them the world over. Chasing the weight.

He buried the Englishman in the night, before the heat got to him, piling a cairn of stones on the mound to keep the dingoes away. In the morning, he climbed down the shaft and saw why the Englishman had stayed, sick or not. The saddlebag was hidden in the shaft wall in a hole packed with mud. The Pole worked for several days, eking out the man's supplies of food and water, until the seam tailed off into the quartz. Then he tidied the camp, leaving no sign that he had been there. He tacked a rough note to the tent ridge pole: Typhoid here taken mate to town. *It worked most times. He'd seen a few with their throat cut for robbing a man's things in his absence. He wrapped the rifle, the revolver and the lettercase in his swag.*

He walked with an easy loping stride across the undulating red earth, through the scrubby acacia trees and the occasional rich green shapeliness of a kurrajong, pausing on a ridge or rocky outcrop to get his bearings, working over in his mind the past days as he went. The Englishman, strangely, had settled in his mind. He thought about him, going over the words written on the thin fraying paper of the letters — the Englishman's life, in a green moist country, growing things, abiding by the seasons; the family letter with the news of his home. The woman waiting for him. She would have given up by now. Taken someone else.

The Pole had been near done in when he'd come on the camp. The Englishman's water and food had saved him, he reckoned, after months on the track, the long stretches without water and the searing temperatures in the ironstone ranges. He'd had a run-in with some blackfellas there. They had made off with his flour and tea and speared his dog, a terrier he'd bought off a mate in Derby.

Cue was busy. Diggers everywhere, crowding the hotels on both sides of the main street. Loaded drays and a camel train were making ready to leave. The Pole was cautious. Finding a bit of shade against the wall of a building he sat, watching, getting the layout of the town. The fine stone buildings glowed in the sun, imposing and permanent. Law and order had settled in Cue.

He had the twenty pound note in his pocket but decided against using it. Instead, he took some of the small gold nuggets to buy a horse and gear from an Italian who was leaving by coach, and started back for the lease at once. The camp was untouched. He had bought what he needed carefully, asking questions here and there with the wariness of experience. Now, without delay, he packed the saddlebags, taking a few items that would be useful. If he didn't the next digger, or the blacks, would. He thought of heading for

Yalgoo, from there to follow the track down to Geraldton. Most of the diggers coming up the coach track were new to the fields. The old timers, more likely, were heading down from the north to Coolgardie.

On the way back in to Cue, he avoided the hotels and crowds and led the horse around to the end of the main street, to the Japanese bathhouse. He liked the Japanese women, their white impassive faces and their silken flesh, the fluttering movements and the vivid colours of their kimonos and sashes. They were familiar to him. He had found them in Tokyo and Santiago and Alaska and other places. Everywhere he had been, they had been, sooner or later; a recurrence in the ever-changing pattern of his life. They were like him. Opportunists, drawn like magnets to a place where they might make money, without pretense. They liked him, or, at least, they pretended to. They mistook his pale blue eyes and blond hair and called him Ingrish. Come in Ingrish, they called, and he would surrender to their ministrations. It was a good omen to find them here. He closed his eyes as they poured steaming water over him — their voices twittering above him, thinking of the Englishman, and his woman, the expectations they had shared. Through the spaces between the rough wooden slabs of the wall he could see the Japanese man watching his horse. He had made his bargain: the women, two bottles of arrack and watch the horse. He kept the revolver with him.

He had changed his mind about following the track to Geraldton. He'd seen faces he'd recognised. He'd be safer on his own. It went against the code to knock back a mate on the track. They'd remember it.

The days were mild, and he walked the heavy-laden horse at a leisurely pace through great swathes of wildflowers, stretching to the horizon. He had seen it before, when he had jumped ship in Esperance and walked up to the fields. On the third day, he shot a kangaroo and grilled thin strips of the rich meat over the coals. He slept with the saddlebags beside him and the revolver near his hand, but his nights were undisturbed. He could feel his strength coming back.

The country, after he left Sandstone, was green and fresh after rain. Flocks of ducks rose from the fringes of the lakes he skirted. He spent time and too many bullets shooting a couple. Further south, well away from the mining settlements, he had been visited by a party of blacks who had trailed him for a day or two and he had slept in uneasy snatches. But they had gone on their way when he had fired the rifle.

The country was easy travelling; he had picked a good season. He found water in rock pools and camped occasionally in a grove of gums, the trunks of the trees as white as snow. It reminded him, faintly, the memory almost extinguished, of a place; snow falling, touching his face, the stamp of boots and the smell of horses, the cold of long dark nights and ... hunger. Somewhere in the north of Europe. He no longer knew where, or cared. It had been so long ago. He had been at sea since he was a boy, adrift on the oceans. Like others of his kind, his memory was as clean and smooth as a pebble on a beach. He belonged nowhere. He belonged to no one but himself. Everyplace or anyplace was the same.

But now he had the saddlebags, heavy with gold. The Englishman's cache and what he had taken himself, in a country huge and empty where, he had seen, men could get land. Men like himself. Scavengers. Drifters. He knew himself and he knew the world and he was weary of it. Walking steadily by day, through the endless drifts of flowers, in the mild sunshine sweet with pollen, he began to toy with the idea of innocence. An innocent life — in this innocent country. He began to dream. The Englishman's dream, as the woman had described it in her letter. At night he wrapped himself in the Englishman's blanket and thought of what he might do.

In Coolgardie he felt safer in the crowded streets, but still he was wary. There were many banks and he took his time choosing each one he entered. He had taken a room in a boarding house where he could stable the horse and carry the saddlebags to his room unnoticed. In the morning he visited a barber and bought clothing and new boots, throwing the others into a pile of rubbish. He went to a hotel and ate a meal, sitting alone at a table. All the time he was thinking of what he had to do next and keeping a sharp eye on the crowd.

The Pole took with him the letter which carried the woman's address in London and the Englishman's gold. It was easier than he had expected. Everyone was too busy to ask too many questions. He waited while the gold was weighed and the papers were drawn up for him to sign. With a calm hand he wrote the scrawl that he had practised in his room. Thomas Drewe. The woman might never receive it. She might be dead. It didn't matter. He considered it a fair price. He didn't need all the dead man's gold. He had taken what he wanted.

He visited the second bank the following day and completed his business, drawing a cash draft against the gold he deposited, signing the name easily, without hesitation. He sold the horse and rifle to the boarding house proprietor and gave his swag to the stablehand. In his new portmanteau he packed the revolver and the lettercase and the articles he had bought. He had visited another barber and had his beard shaved off and now, in the cracked mirror propped on a shelf, he looked at himself and tried on his hat, tilting it a little. He had not seen himself for a long time. The face was strange. Thomas Drewe's face. He put the train ticket in the pocket of his new coat and left, nodding his head in farewell to the proprietor as he passed through the door.

He found a seat on the crowded train and waited for the departure time. He opened the newspaper he had bought and held it up in front of him, although he doubted that anyone who knew the Big Pole would recognise him. He was going south. He was finished with the gold. He was finished with the sea. He was going to get himself some land and stay there. The train jerked and began to move out of the town, through the Flat crowded with tents and hessian houses, out into the bush, a sea of gold against the red earth, the air sweet with the tang of wattle. A memory came to him. Vivid and clear. A peach tree in full blossom, its boughs spreading wide. Somewhere — once — there had been a peach tree.

The Rock

Lasseter Highway was a straight black line dissecting the red dunes. Sculpted in curves and arcs; balanced by the perfect placement of a desert oak, a tangle of wind-bent mulga. Pared to the ultimate bare line; a minimal elegance of geometrical precision.

Zoe asked Tom to stop. 'I have to try and photograph them.'

'It's wasting time,' he said, but he pulled off onto a lookout point for Mount Connor. The monolith floated on the horizon, the view that first-time travellers always mistake for Ayers Rock. Zoe scrambled out of the cab and crossed the road quickly. A track led up the incline of a dune. Thousands had been here before her but the dunes remained intact.

At the crest, a blaze of light forced her to shield her eyes. A hard white glare, stretching to the horizon. Lake Amadeus. She tried to see through the shimmer. Mirages were forming;

shapes, flowing and changing. A train of camels etched a line, spidery legs fine drawn under cumbersome bodies. The stick figures of lost explorers, goldseekers, the landhungry, held captive in the mud under the thin salt crust. Forever caught in the inferno of the sun. Close to the perimeter, black elongated shadows angled out, motionless; watching.

The blaze of light had blurred her sight. Quickly she took photographs, snatching at frames, the imprints on her retina: form and colour. Shape and balance. The place was too powerful.

Back in the truck she closed her eyes waiting for the red haze to subside, her pulse beating rapidly with the heat and exertion.

At Curtin Springs, a neat grey-haired traveller chatted to Tom while he was refuelling, warning him to get to Yulara by late afternoon.

'The Abos buy grog here. The wife and I had a close shave on the way in. A carload nearly ran us off the road.'

His wife nodded. 'They can buy it here, and they're drunk when they leave.'

'A difficult problem,' Zoe murmured. The woman sniffed.

'Watch out,' the man had called as they left. 'The tourist coaches are fast and they don't leave much room.'

They reached Yulara at dusk. Too tired to take it in, they followed signposts past the white sails and rigging suspended in the evening sky, past landscaped gardens and car parks and a bewildering complex of buildings. They found the caravan park and a bay hedged in by shrubs, and were thankful for the comfort of electricity, a hot shower and rest.

Familiar sounds woke them early: men talking and laughing on the way back from early showers, a truck doing the rounds of rubbish collection. The aroma of breakfasts cooking filtered into the van. Zoe pulled the curtain back and let the morning light in. The colours were strong, singular, without sub tones: the earth, cadmium scarlet, she decided; the sky, cerulean, unmarred by cloud. In the desert bushes, raucous birds dived and foraged for food, ignoring passers-by.

They sat inside the van to eat their breakfast. This, Zoe thought, is a morning like no other. We've reached the heart; the legendary Rock. A delicate balance, she knew, stretched between her and Tom; the aftermath of disturbances they had, as yet, not acknowledged. Strangeness and the extraordinary had taken residence with them. In the brief code of people who have lived together for a long time, they signalled an agreement to postpone confronting it. They tidied the van and shook out clean clothes, performing minor rituals in preservation of the surface.

It was mid-morning by the time they were ready to go out. Already the heat was in the ascendancy, slowing their movements. Their steps matched the languor of others moving around the pathways. In the shopping centre they mingled with tourists, the excited chatter of groups of Japanese students and the gutturals of older Germans sitting around the cafes more frequent than the sound of English. The young employees in their resort uniform of tailored shorts and shirts were attractive, friendly and well-trained; the tourist was nurtured. *Ayers Rock*, a poster said, *a Premium Destination*. In a gift shop a black cockatoo feather had a miniature of the Rock painted in brilliant colours, and a price tag in the high hundreds. Everywhere the icon of the Rock confronted them with the purpose of their visit. In the narrow alleyways between apartment blocks, hedges of shrubbery and vines softened the density of accommodation. Turned in on itself, the resort focused on the tourists who had come to see the Rock in the desert. There was no other reason. The Rock and the Olgas were the lifeblood of the resort.

Tom and Zoe were part of it. On the twenty-two kilometre drive to the National Park they joined a stream of buses and cars and caravans. It was suddenly there, in front of them. Enormous on the flat plain. Glowing vermilion in the morning sun.

They followed the traffic, looking for a parking space. AAT King's Coaches were disgorging passengers. Groups stood and chatted. Individuals wandered in a daze, heads tilted back, taking photographs.

The campervan fitted into a tight space beside a Brits hire van. In front of the open door, the couple had set up a folding table. They were drinking tea from a thermos and writing postcards.

'Morning,' the man said. 'Going to do the climb?'

'I haven't decided,' Tom told him.

'Good day for it. Not too much wind. Not too hot yet.' His wife nodded. 'What about you love?' he said to Zoe.

'No,' she said. 'I didn't come here for that.'

'Oh, one of those,' he smiled. '*The traditional owners don't like it.* There was none of that when we were here in '77 was there love?' His wife shook her head under her sun hat. He gathered his postcards into a pile. 'God bless,' he said as they moved on.

'He was just being friendly,' Tom said.

'Are you going to climb it?' she asked.

'I might.'

'Look at them!' Zoe said. The line of climbers stretched out of sight, an endless stream on the immense fall of rock. They walked to the base of the climb and read the warnings, more explicit than usual. A ranger was talking about the dangers of the climb to a group of young backpackers eager to start, telling them not to stray from the chain; of the need to pace themselves. He spoke of the continual accidents and the difficulty and danger of effecting rescues. The ranger let them go, throwing a harassed grin at Tom and Zoe as he moved on.

There was an atmosphere, a tension. Those who were descending were triumphant, or, in some cases, distressed. Those who were beginning the ascent were excited, talking and laughing, encouraging each other. It was infectious; exhilarating.

'I think I'll have a go,' Tom said.

Zoe shrugged. 'You don't have to prove anything.'

Tom took off his hat and combed his grey-blond hair back with his fingers, a familiar gesture of preparation. 'Good luck,' she said, and restrained herself from adding *be careful*. He climbed easily and rapidly, his lean frame and muscular legs were graceful in movement. He was the Australian male women loved to love she thought. Strong, capable, even sensitive ... but impenetrable. After so long — despite what he had revealed at the Canyon — he remained impenetrable. She tried to imagine the boy's bleak loneliness and unhappiness — his grief and guilt for his father. It was unfathomable that he had never told her — that he had not trusted her. She had known him most of his life. She remembered a day when he had been vulnerable; lying in the grass near the river, the Madden girls teasing him, taunting him. She had straddled his body to hold him down while her sisters tickled him with grass stems, their breasts hanging over him.

She had felt his sex move under her. He had tossed her off and gone. Diving into the river, embarrassed and angry. Her sisters had laughed and she had been angry with them, allying herself with him. He hadn't come back for some time after that. He'll be back, her sisters had said, sure of their power. But she had not been so sure. He was different when she returned after the years at university. His father was dead. He never talked of his family. She saw now that her protectiveness had been an element in her feeling for him.

Zoe watched Tom climb steadily and rhythmically amongst the other climbers, losing definition as he gained height. In the effort of keeping him in sight, his body had become a blur, dissolving, like a futurist painting, into the angles and planes of his movement. He was remote from her, unreachable. She would paint him like that ... some time. Disassemble him into lines and contours. Somewhere in the composition she would find the opening; the impervious skin would be no defense. She would know everything about him. She shivered slightly in the sun, aware that there was a coldness in her will to pursue him that way. There was a danger in objectivity.

Endlessly, the crowd toiled up the Rock, the figures becoming indistinct specks of colour. Perspective and meaning splintered into atoms; the red walls of stone overwhelming the minute bodies clinging to the chain hammered into its surface. Zoe felt the urge to shatter the icon; the bizarre notion that the essence of the Centre could be attained in such a way. If she were to paint it, it would be this ... procession: the ascent, a *Mecca*. A kind of *carnivale* surrounding it. Women with coloured sweat bands and stretch shorts, men with joggers and muscles oiled and gleaming, prancing in readiness. Diminutive Japanese women with parasols decorated with cherry blossoms (why not; every symbol had its place). The starving dingo pups — lean as Florentine hounds — driven in from the desert in search of food, mingling with the crowd. She watched a stretch limousine arrive, disgorging its privileged cargo dressed in white. The group strolled to the base of the Rock, preceded by their driver clearing a way, a mobile telephone held to his ear. The hierarchy of power. The chain on the Rock — the people on the chain, the chain of climbers ... But — there was a darkness behind the colour and movement. From the shadowed pockmarks and cavities in the Rock, eyes would watch. Disembodied eyes following the climbers toiling to achieve the summit. There would have to be a fall. Death, after all, was a constant presence in the desert, at the Rock; the baby taken (Meryl Streep should never have attempted the Australian accent) unleashing a dark brutality across the country. Death: stalking the climbers, the wanderers, the unaware; Kurrpanngu, the fearsome dingo spirit dreamed into being by the Wintalka men to punish the Mala? No. She wouldn't dare. She would stick with what she knew: death by falling, thirst, fright — obsession: Lasseter ... delusion ... the woman tourist left behind in Katherine Gorge, found dead the next morning — unable to withstand the sheer fright of being left alone in such a place. And the plain from which the Rock rose would be the blood-red that it truly was, and the trees would have stems of bleached bone: *the leg bone connected to the thigh bone, the thigh bone connected to the hip bone and that's the word of the Lord.* Yes, apocryphal, because when they got there, the summit was bare. There was nothing there for them. They would see themselves surrounded by emptiness.

It came to her — simply. Her paintings of the valley — the delicate impressions, the skilful playing with light and shade, the evocations of seasonal change — were chimera, floating on her retina, pre-supposed elsewhere. The drifts of colour when the fruit trees were in blossom, the soft green hills, all tenderness and nurture, were landscapes of the transforming eye; nostalgia for an unknown otherworld. Other people's exile. The generations passed it on, no longer knowing the source of their vision; no longer having the words for it. They travelled *north* to find the sun, looking, looking everywhere. Unconscious of the tragic error in their internal compass they circled the continent, carrying the dislocation of their ancestry with them.

The coach drivers chatted and smoked while they waited for their passengers to return. It was routine for them, endlessly repeated; a *Premier Destination*. Zoe wandered over to talk to them, curious as to what they would say.

They were friendly, willing to break the monotony of waiting; careful in their comments. The Japanese travelled in groups, they told her. A day at Ayers Rock and a week to do Australia, usually. They were ideal passengers, uncomplaining, enthusiastic. The young backpackers, mostly Germans, Swedes, Danes, Americans — travelled light, asked questions, saw everything. 'And the traditional owners?' she asked.

Stayed out of the way. Tolerated the tourists, but didn't particularly want to mix with them. They weren't happy about the Mingas, the ants, doing the climb. Too dangerous.

They take groups on walks, sure, the Mala Walk, the fertility cave, the Liru Walk, but they only tell you what they want you to know. They keep to themselves ...

'The dollar sign is the most sacred thing around here,' a

driver said, brushing his immaculate uniform free of invisible dust.

The group broke up. Passengers were returning. They had a schedule to maintain. A passenger manifest to check. Tensions ...

Zoe wandered off towards the path that led to the base of the Rock, timing it so that she trailed a guided group through a scattering of slender trees and shrubs up towards the cave. Families would have camped here, sheltered from sun and storms. Preparing for the ceremonies. The roof of the cave was blackened with smoke. On the wall there were drawings and cryptic signs: of water? or messages of food supplies, game? A rock in front of the drawings was a convenient sitting place. A man might have sat there and made drawings while his children played outside and his wife pounded seeds, or sat at a fire, the smoke rising in a thin spiral curling around the stone above her. A hundred years ago, a thousand, five thousand ... Zoe's skin prickled. Here was where the life was. Down here. Close to the earth. Where the Rock and the earth joined. The space of the cave was dense with the memory of people, their voices and movements and vitality. The rubble and dust on the floor carried the traces. She touched the walls, knowing that in the logicality of history, men and women had touched there also, leaving, as she did, the invisible imprint of her presence.

She followed the path past the cave, the dark powerful opening of the hare-wallaby's pouch — where access was barred — through the trees into the enclosing high walls of Kantju Gorge. The stone was carved into deep furrows by rain channelled into the pool; a water supply. A sacred place of men's ceremony. It was cool in the shade of the trees and the stone walls, and she lingered. She became aware of a crowding around her, slight at first, then becoming uncomfortable. She shook her head but the sensation persisted, an insistent unmistakeable pressure. Personas — masculine, curious — were probing at her. At her mind. She couldn't stay — it was too powerful. Too much had been enacted. Something was still here. She held her palms against her head, the pulse of blood too fast.

She hurried on the path until she saw a group ahead of her. Out in the sun the heat struck at her but she shivered, her skin chilled. Cicadas sang in the grass, loud — louder. The guide was explaining. Here was the cave where Tjati died, the man, the red lizard. She had tried to grasp the stories, to place them in her mind. She had read Robert Layton's account again and again before she left home, trying to memorise the Tjukurrpa law which was the evidence of ownership, but the reality was overpowering. The dizzying sweep and fall of stone loomed over her; the skin of the Rock, holed and pockmarked, cracked and fissured by the passage and action of legendary Beings. It was too much to know. The sun beat down on her. The cicadas increased their tempo to a frantic whirr ... She had not expected an insight — no Yankjuntjatara or Pitjantjatjara elder would appear and give her special dispensation to understand. It was arrogant to expect it. There were two realities and she inhabited one of them. What she allowed as a possibility was this exposure of herself to what was in the air, the stone, the water; to what remained — beyond reason. But it was too much for her. Exhausted, she walked slowly, with her head down, back along the road. Buses and cars passed her, doing the circuit of the Rock. Soon she would be back at the truck. Behind her a dingo padded, thirsty and hungry.

Tom could see Zoe sitting in the truck, waiting for him.

What could he tell her? That, while he was up there, he had realised the centre was too far in for him? Between him and his own place the desert stretched interminably. He had decided not to sign the visitors' book; he felt no sense of victory. The summit had done nothing for him.

As soon as his calf muscles had recovered, he had begun the descent.

He had made the decision to go to the goldfields. He would look for Dubrovic, for Drewe, for some trace ... find out. He had put it off for too long.

They rested and slept through the heat of the afternoon, the small fan blowing a steady draft of warm air over them. When they awoke the sky had clouded over, wind-driven cumulus were piling and building.

'We could get some rain out of this,' Tom said, peering through the window. 'It's coming from the north-west. Could be the tail-end of a cyclone.'

After the months of travelling through hot parched country and the recurring thunderstorms, the thought of rain and coolness was irresistible. They stayed. They slept late the next morning, visited the supermarket and bought fresh food for a hot meal. In the newsagency, Zoe lingered. As well as the major Australian daily papers there were international papers: *Le Monde, Corriere Della Sera, Berliner Zeitung, Tokyo Shimbun* and the *New Straits Times* had front page articles on Australia. There were maps, photos of Aboriginal leaders. Several Australian papers carried front page stories about another Native Title battle in the Supreme Court. Wik. The short word stuck in her mind. What had been happening — while they were travelling around, out of touch. The attendant gave her a quizzical look when she paid him for the papers she'd selected.

'I want to catch up,' she said.

Tom had gone out walking. She sat at the table with the papers spread around her, taking sides, wanting to believe there had been a change ... Hoping it would hold.

There was novelty in being alone. Zoe took a long shower, shampooing her hair and twisting it up in a knot. She soaked her skin in moisturiser, reflecting on the personal routines they had shed without noticing. She had not had a haircut for three months, Tom had grown a beard. It was weeks since she had looked in a mirror. Now, when she had the chance, she didn't want to look, as if self-consciousness would be a distraction; the mirrored image would pull her back, reconnect her to her ordinary life. There was the smell of rain in the air. The workers around the camping grounds had placed signs: *no camping — nature at work*. The temperature had dropped twenty degrees overnight, allowing a return of energy. The occupants of the few caravans travelling this late in the season were busy checking gear, washing down vehicles. Savouring the coolness, Zoe sat down to write postcards before Tom returned. Hurrying to finish so she could post them at the kiosk.

She wrote to her daughter:

> *Dearest Mim: arrived at Uluru two days ago. Aboriginal culture is the drawcard, but the people themselves are invisible. Bought newspapers today, first time for weeks. They are full of Native Title paranoia. The land question brings out the worst in this country. Travelling around it is disturbing. Hope you are safe and well. Much Love. Please write. Z.*

She missed her daughter, the need to talk was pressing on her. Dutifully, she wrote to the rest of her family:

164

Dear Sophie, having a cool change at Ayers Rock. It has been hot travelling. Wonderful red sand dunes. This is Lake Amadeus. Shades of Mozart in the desert! From here we'll be heading home. Hope you are handling the winter. Love Z.

Dear Jeremy, Liz, Kitty and Ben. As you can see we are still in Central Australia. Although there are more international people here than Australians. Tom climbed the Rock. I didn't. We'll keep in touch. Heading south tomorrow. Love to all. Z.

Late in the day Zoe made sandwiches and a thermos of coffee. It was fifty-odd kilometres to the Olgas. They drove as fast as they could, caught in the stream of traffic heading to the Rock for the sunset. The domed massif of the Olgas loomed at a turn in the road; the exotic formations were all curves and folds, the openings in dark shadow. They passed the turn-off to Docker River and Western Australia.

'Lasseter died out there. The cave must be close to the road, it's marked on the map — a tourist attraction.' Zoe pointed to the road sign. 'We could turn there and go home, take a short cut.'

'Let's do it,' Tom said. 'Tomorrow. We'd be home in a few days.'

'No.' Zoe was abrupt. 'No, we're not ready.'

Tom looked at her. 'You mightn't be ...'

They left it. The Olgas were suddenly in front of them. They sat watching the stream of people from coaches entering and leaving the gorge.

'We'll have to make a move,' Tom said, 'the light will be going shortly.'

They walked together into the shadow of the gorge, subdued by the grandeur. The wind had become stronger, vibrating and echoing through the deep passage between the walls, unnerving in its pitch and intensity. There was no sense of exhilaration here, no excitement. Other walkers, like themselves, were reduced by the strange towering curved walls. People walked soberly, their voices muted. At the end of the gorge there was a barrier; a narrow passage continued beyond it overgrown with vegetation. A sign requested that visitors not proceed. There was no explanation; the owners withheld the mystery. No one attempted to explore beyond the barrier; the usual brash curiosity was subdued. When they returned to the car park the sun had gone. Coach parties, buffeted by the gusting wind, were gathered around the Sunset Champagne and Barbecue parties they had paid for. Dark cloud was closing in rapidly. There was no refund for the failed sunset.

In the dusk, they drove back to the viewing platform. The parking area was empty. The metal walkway wound up the side of a dune to the platform. They sat on one of the deserted benches to share their supper. Protected by the dune, the air was soft and warm. In front of them was an open woodland of desert oak, delicate ink brushstrokes against the Olgas, soft violet in the evening light, a mist or haze of dust settling around the base.

Tom broke the silence. 'They are named after the Queen of Spain.'

'Kata Tjuta,' Zoe replied. 'A queen of Spain has nothing to do with this.'

A breath of air moved around them, the last of the day's heat; the land's release. 'It's a strange thing, to belong to a country and be excluded from its secret life.'

The desert oaks had blurred into a shadow and only the faintest outline of the mountains was visible. Stillness settled over the landscape; a pause before the activity of the night.

'We have no reverence for it, that's what's missing,' Zoe said. 'We've substituted a sense of endurance. We test our strength *against* it.'

'It's the way we are,' Tom said.

His profile was in silhouette; insubstantial and remote.

'What is it Tom?' Zoe felt his breathing change — his resistance. A wave of frustration compelled her. 'What's troubling you? Why can't you say what it is?' The silence stretched and she felt a moment of panic.

'Sometimes it is what you do that matters,' he said, 'not words.'

'What do you mean?'

'It's nothing.' He stood up, capping the thermos flask, gathering the sandwich wrapping.

Nothing ... She knew better than to persist. In the faint light of the moon behind the moving cloud they found their way down the walkway, the night air heavy with moisture wrapping around them. 'It will rain tonight,' Tom said, leading the way. They groped their way to the car as the moon moved behind cloud.

Zoe waited for him to unlock the car. 'I've never felt such loneliness.'

'There's nothing to harm us here,' he said.

'I know that,' she replied. 'I'm not afraid of the land.'

They passed the turn-off to Docker River without comment. Driving back to the resort, they made no effort at conversation. At Yulara, lights blazed in the cafes and people wandered along pathways and roadways in the warm stillness of the night. Music could be heard, and compressors in giant refrigeration trucks parked in loading bays hummed in the background. It was an outpost in space; a colony with a purpose.

Reluctant to return to the enclosed intimacy of the campervan, they sat and ate linguini at an Italian restaurant and watched the crowd.

'Notice anything?' Zoe said, indicating the busy scene.

'What?'

'No Yankuntjatjara, no Pitjantjatjara. Not one.'

They strolled across the grass to the luxurious foyer of the hotel and looked through the art gallery. A white artist sat painting brilliant miniatures of the Rock. Large paintings of master Aboriginal artists were elegantly hung and subtly lit. Pearls from Broome, diamonds from Argyle, gleamed in display cabinets. The carved lizards and snakes created for the tourist trade writhed in corners. Raku pots, simulating the flaking ochre of the Rock, stood alone under a spotlight. The prices were out of their range. In the cosmopolitan marketplace they were shabby in their shorts and sandals; without status. The elegant attendant ignored them. In a small amphitheatre a didgeridoo played and figures moved on a large screen; the story of the Dreamtime being played out ... nightly, for a moderate charge.

During the night Zoe awoke. Dingoes were howling out in the desert. Tom was not in bed and she listened to the eerie, wild sound, waiting for him to return. The wind had risen again, a bin lid rolled and clattered. The van shook slightly with the gusts. Tom came in and she could smell the damp on him. 'It's raining,' he said. 'Seems to be setting in.'

She held the sheet aside for him, moving close for the comfort of his presence. His skin was cool and sweet with rain.

They rose in the dark and made coffee and toast. It was still raining, a steady light rain, already making pools on the parched earth and freshening the vegetation. By the time they reached the Rock, a grey dawn was breaking. Cloud hung low over the crest. The Rock was changed. Magenta-burgundy; sombre and sublime. Deserted at this hour.

Zoe left Tom wandering along the base and walked across the road into the bush. It was a deception, a brief imaginary flight into the interior. She walked softly on the rose-madder earth, avoiding the silver-tipped spinifex, her back to the Rock; acting out the pretense that she was alone. When she turned, finally, the summit of the Rock was wrapped in cloud, a rain mist drifting across it. There was no sound or movement around her. In the dawn stillness she sat on the ground, breaking the thin crust with her body weight. Her hands, lean and brown, rested against the delicate pink skin, fine as silk under her fingers. Relaxed, unmoving, she waited ... This is how it is, she thought. Expecting nothing. Being patient. Waiting, out here — on the edge. She witnessed the timeless act of transfer; the taking in of moisture, the giving out of heat; the cycle of nurture and renewal. She stayed in the seclusion of the trees and shrubs, watching the cloud descending into the gullies and fissures where unnameable forces resided, drawing a soft trail of vapour over the face of the Rock. She smiled. The land spoke in metaphors, brief and subtle, but she had caught it. Tomorrow it would again be crowded with climbers, the postcard icon: red ochre under a brilliant blue sky and a hot sun.

The light steady rain had soaked her jacket. She began the walk back, refreshed and at ease.

The buses had arrived. A disconsolate group of tourists clustered around the base of the climb. 'No sunset last night and no climb this morning,' an American said. 'I'm only here for one day. Can you believe it?' A ranger was fielding inquiries ... explaining the danger of slipping on the wet rock. An elderly woman sat on a bench, a red umbrella shielding her from the rain. A pair of dingo puppies sat at her feet, hoping for food. A girl photographed them.

A LandCruiser pulled in alongside their truck and the Aboriginal driver sat watching the scene. Tom greeted him. 'Do you think there'll be enough rain for a run-off?'

'No,' the man said, 'wash the dust off, that's about all.'

'They don't look too happy about it,' Tom said, indicating the group of tourists.

'It's too dangerous to climb. These people haven't got a clue. Most of them are on a day trip.' Both men grinned, sharing the moment. 'Are you from around here?' Tom asked.

'I work here, but I'm from the west.'

'So are we,' Tom said, 'the south.'

'Broome,' the man said in response.

'We're on the way back.'

'My daughter's down there.'

'Well, we're off,' Tom said. They nodded to each other.

'I'm hungry,' Zoe said, 'I'm going to cook breakfast before we leave.'

'Good idea,' Tom agreed. 'We better stock up a bit too. There's nothing much between here and Port Augusta.'

Going South

Going South

Leaving was simpler than arriving, but not casual. While they stayed at a place they relaxed a little, spread out. The longer they stayed the more space they used, their belongings stowed under the truck, towels hung on folding chairs outside, outdoor shoes lined up beside the door. Packing up was also a tightening up. They moved quicker, spoke in abrupt sentences, concentrating on preparing the van and the truck for travelling. A good trip depended on forgetting nothing. Disconnecting the power line and stowing the long length of extension cord was the point at which they ended the experience. After that, there was nothing left to do but go.

Each departure had its own particular atmosphere; of reluctance, relief, anticipation. Driving out onto Lasseter Highway, Zoe was subdued. Tom, in the mood for a stretch of driving, was cheerful. A tourist coach passed them, turning in at the road to the airport.

'Another planeload of tourists,' Zoe said. 'Every day the same.'

She fished in her bag and found the packet of photographs she had collected from the photo studio. Amongst them was the view of the Rock which Gosse had sketched in 1873: the abrupt western end, the striations on the wall, the clump of trees at ground level. It was instantly recognisable. She had taken it in the morning light, not realising she had captured the same angle.

'Look at this,' she said, propping it on the dashboard in front of Tom. 'The same view as the Gosse sketch — a hundred years later. That's how I'll remember it.'

'Maybe you could enlarge it,' Tom said, 'duplicate Gosse's sketch.'

'I might.'

'Have a look at the map,' he asked her, 'see how far it is to Marla.'

Zoe folded the map. 'Almost five hundred, will we make that tonight? What's at Marla?'

'Nothing, as far as I know. It's just a stop to make for. Tomorrow, if we start early we could be in Port Augusta.'

'It's over isn't it?' Zoe said.

'What's over?'

'The exploration.'

'We've got a long way to go yet.'

'Yes, but the ... search is over. We never found the Golden Boomerang. When Peggy grew up I bet she became an anthropologist and went to — to the Trobriands or Java and wrote books.'

'And Tuckonie?'

'He worked — on a cattle station — then went to Alice Springs.'

'And the grog got him —'

'No — not Tuckonie. He went back to his country and became famous as a painter and spokesman for his people.'

'Land rights I suppose. Is that a happy ending for a fairy story?'

'The proper ending for a fairy story is that they got married and lived happily ever after ...' She rummaged in the cassettes and found the Tchaikovsky Collection. *The Dance of the Sugar Plum Fairies* filled the cab.

'Do you have to play that?'

'It's a gesture,' she said, 'a farewell — to innocence.'

'Innocence?' Tom asked.

'Mine,' she replied. 'My child's view — my interior landscape.'

Surprisingly, he agreed with her.

They passed Mount Ebenezer roadhouse again. A group of people were still sitting under the tree. The scene seemed unchanged. 'Do you want to stop?' Tom asked. 'They do the animal carvings here and sell direct to the tourist buses.'

'Not now. If we'd known on the way in ... Ebenezer ... Who was it, I wonder, who walked this country with the Old Testament in one hand and a surveying staff in the other?'

'Now Israel went out to battle against the Philistines,' she chanted, *'they encamped at Ebenezer and the Philistines encamped at Aphek. The Philistines drew up in line against Israel, and when the battle spread, Israel was defeated by the Philistines.'*

'How did you know that?'

'Athol. He knew all about the Philistines. Except then, *we* were the Israelites and the rest were the Philistines I guess. Now we are the Philistines, and Aboriginal people are the Israelites; outcasts in their own country.'

'Mabo has changed that.'

'Terra Nullius! What supreme arrogance ... to justify taking land. Anyway, the Wik claim is the big one.'

'Landholders will fight tooth and nail ...'

'It's aggressive — putting it like that — *Red in tooth and claw —* '

Tom shrugged. 'Men are aggressive about land.'

'The war zone. Hidden in the heart,' Zoe tapped the map on her knee, 'the central artery lined with war bases.'

They had passed several *No Entry* signs indicating restricted military area. Gravel roads leading into the bush. And somewhere between Katherine and Alice Springs they had stumbled onto that abandoned World War Two airfield. The experience had been unnerving.

'Think of it,' she said, 'the population clustered on the coastline, unaware of this central artery pumping the war machine.'

'We were a country at war, remember, in danger of being invaded. It was the only access to the north.'

'But the civilian population was on the coast. The centre was virtually empty.'

'You don't know what you're talking about. It's barren country. It couldn't support a large population.'

'Not too barren for war games. And eagles,' she added. Again and again they had passed huge wedgetail eagles hunched over the torn bodies of animals caught on the highway. Their immense wing spans curved over their prey; a massive talon sunk in the flesh. 'Raptors,' Zoe said. 'Everything is drawn to the highway — even the eagles.'

Tom shrugged. 'Easy pickings. I wonder what Athol would say about defence, with his famous pacifist ideas.'

'He hated unjust wars,' Zoe replied, but it silenced her. Athol's stance as a pacifist was a delicate subject. His editorials on war had caused him trouble.

Silence and secrecy. Tom had had enough of it. He'd lived with it all his childhood years, overpowered by the forces and tensions that had prowled the house. He had never known where the danger was; the source of the threat was always a mystery to him. For the first time he had put distance between him and the valley. And he could see it ... could see the shadow in which he had moved: his grandfather, most of all, the powerful personality, dominating the household. He could not imagine what he might have been in the absence of his grandfather. He would talk to Athol now, if he was still alive. Athol had known something — had known, and said nothing. Rattling linotype in his pocket, throwing the metal symbols on the table like a seer reading bones. Perhaps he hadn't understood that he, Tom, was in the dark.

They reached Erldunda, at the intersection of the highway, and turned right. It was lunchtime but they didn't stop. Without discussion, the tempo of the journey had changed. They were pushing on, no longer sightseers but travellers intent on reaching the end of their journey. They had a tailwind once they turned south.

'We should make it to Marla with this wind,' Tom said. 'We can fuel up there.'

Strong gusts whipped the scrub lining the road, adding to the sense of propulsion. To Zoe, it seemed that gravity was pushing them southwards, down to the coast; as if the weight of the continent was behind them.

They stopped briefly at the South Australian border for a hurried snack, huddled in the campervan amongst the jerrycans of water and other equipment stowed for travelling. The country around them was flat and inhospitable under a grey sky.

'Looks like the weather is following us down,' Tom said.

'It's hard to believe the change,' Zoe said. 'All the colour has gone — the clarity.'

No wonder people keep coming back, she thought. The inner life: You could hunger for it. Inexpressible, incommunicable. It was an intrinsic part of the revelation; the brief moment of fusion and the grief of separation.

To live in that way, in a deep harmony with one's country, and be wrenched from it with a sudden violence was almost impossible to contemplate. The shock waves of pain and alienation reverberating for generations. The search for lost children. The severed connections; the aftermath of any war ... Todd River ... ghosts. The incredible thing was — it was still there. The life; the land pulsed with it. The continuum of memory intact in the earth itself, in stone and tree and water. They knew that — of course — the people who came from there. But the survivors — who didn't know where they came from — how would they feel?

'It's depressing,' Zoe said, rinsing the dregs of her coffee mug and recapping the thermos.

'It'll fine up,' Tom said, assuming she meant the weather.

The monotonous landscape unfolded, kilometre after kilometre. Zoe dozed, slipping in and out of half-waking dreams; anxieties and resonances. Tom and Jeremy — they were so alike; there was always tension between them. Mim, so *long* since she had written. Zoe had supported her daughter's flight from home, but so far away ... and such dangerous causes. The postcards with the World Health Organisation logo came from places that frightened Zoe and worried Tom. 'I've got to get away while I can,' she'd said. 'This place is like a drug, it's deadening.' She'd been right, Zoe thought (although she hadn't thought it then). She thought of the valley, the air heavy with nectar; sweet and somnolent.

Awake, Zoe offered to drive. Tom insisted he was all

right. He preferred to drive, but she made the offer on long stretches anyway.

Tom drove at a steady pace, the wind constant behind them. Road trains roared past, shaking the campervan. Caravans heading north passed them in slow convoys, battling the fierce headwind. Occasional showers of rain spattered the windscreen, making rivulets of mud out of the dust. It was raining steadily when they reached Marla. The small caravan park was full. The harassed owner of the roadhouse was unsympathetic: 'Your best bet is Coober Pedy.' They paid for fuel and queued for hot potato chips and coffee amongst Aboriginal teenagers playing video games on the verandah.

The windscreen wipers made a monotonous scratch across the screen as they drove towards Coober Pedy. On either side white cones of mullock marked excavations and drill holes. Signs warned of the danger of leaving the road. The white hillocks stretched as far as they could see; a desolate lunar landscape, without relief. They drove into the townsite, looking for somewhere to stop. Heavy-duty vehicles passed them in a spray of water and mud. People huddled in the shelter of buildings. In this brutal setting, ugliness was a heavy stamp on everything. The thought that the life was subterranean, and as brutal as the environment, was intimidating. Without stopping, they turned around and drove away.

Zoe was peering at the map. 'There's a camping area about eighty kilometres further on.'

'That will have to be it,' Tom said.

The campsite was on a rise, bare except for a few pines, bent and twisted by the wind. There were signs that road trains used the site: deep muddy wheel ruts, and the charcoal smudges of old campfires. With darkness falling, Tom inched along a track looking for some shelter in the lee of the hill. They parked finally near a clump of tired vegetation, an overflowing rubbish bin and a cluster of rocks which did duty as a fireplace. The ugliness and litter spoke of carelessness and overuse.

During the night the roar of motors and the hiss of airbrakes woke them as trucks pulled in. In the morning the campsite was empty.

It was as if they had shifted into a different dimension, bleached of colour. The wind was cold, penetrating their light clothing. Zoe rummaged in a bag, dragging out jumpers and coats. Their mood matched the weather. She dug out the Walkman and adjusted the earphones. Voices filled her head ... instruments of wind and breath, disembodied: *Credo in unum Deo Omnipotens ... Palestrina ...* Fifteenth-century music, in a language she barely understood, singing what had been her core belief: one powerful God in an unchanging universe. The sound suited the bleak worn nubs of mountain ranges, the bare pale stretches of windswept plains. Voices chanting against the emptiness. She thought of Fregon. Out there somewhere on the border: a closed community of Pitjantjatjara where the women painted the internal view of their country, designs unlike anything she had seen before; a tight coherence of being. She closed her eyes. She was homesick. For no particular place. Homesick for a place she hadn't found yet.

Overnight the wind had swung around to the south, reducing the speed at which the top-heavy campervan was comfortable to drive. The truck moved steadily along the highway. On either side salt lakes stretched to the horizon, impassable and cruel. To find yourself stranded out there, Tom thought, would kill the mind and the body. Yet Stuart had found his way around it. What kind of men submitted themselves to such ordeals? He was aware that he was preparing himself for what was ahead. He had no clear plan as yet, only the understanding that his life had lost substance. The valley had become unreal, floating in his imagination, filled with echoes and memories. *Now* was real and personal. The vibration of the truck motor, the dials registering the fuel consumption, the temperature, the oil pressure; the tension in his back muscles and legs. The real world had narrowed to the confines of the cab.

Zoe woke briefly. 'Where are we?' she asked.

'I've no idea,' he said. 'We're about halfway.'

It was an interval without decisions, following the road, the destination locked in. When the highway ended they would be there.

Port Augusta was stormbound. Heavy drenching rain fell on deserted streets. The harbour water was a steely grey, flecked with foam. There was a tight neatness about the caravan park. Manicured lawns and dense clipped shrubbery guided them into the administration centre. Signs were everywhere: *No Unattended Children at the Pool, No Visitors Cars Beyond the Barrier, No Cycling or Skating on Pathways. No Pets.* Caravans were closed against the weather, television aerials networked under the Norfolk pines.

After a hot shower they ate a mixed grill in the restaurant. The neatly attired patrons — middle-aged, not-talking — gazed out the windows. Without the buoyancy of movement, the excitement and adventure of *Going Around Australia* evaporated. The travellers waited for good weather, stranded in a state of boredom and indecision.

Tom and Zoe waited in line to use the telephone. They spoke briefly to Jeremy, exchanging the trite phrases of location, well-being and family news. The rain had eased and they took a brief stroll along the foreshore before returning to the van, damp and irritable. It was too wet to leave anything outside and the small interior space was cluttered with bags.

'I think I'll go to bed and read,' Zoe said. 'There's nothing else to do.'

Tom was restless. 'I can't go to bed yet.' He left Zoe in bed reading. He was gone some time.

'Where have you been?' she asked when he returned.

He filled the kettle and plugged it in. 'Like a cup of coffee?'

She sat up in bed sipping the coffee, a blanket piled around her.

'What's happening,' she said. 'What are we doing?'

He hesitated, tapping his coffee mug, not looking at her.

'Where were you?'

'I was waiting to telephone Jeremy again.'

'Is something wrong?'

'No, no. They're all right.' Waves were breaking on the foreshore in rapid heavy succession, eating into the dunes. He had walked there after he had spoken to Jeremy. 'I wanted to ask him if he could stay on for awhile. He's been commuting, stopping a couple of nights in the city and then working from the orchard. Liz and the children have settled in it seems.'

'I thought we were on our way back.' She pulled the blanket tighter.

'There's something I have to tell you, Zoe — should have told you before ... It concerns Jeremy too, that's why I asked him to stay on.'

She waited for Tom to speak.

'It's to do with the land — the title.'

She was motionless, watching him.

'I don't know if there's a problem, but I have to try and find out.'

'What kind of a problem?'

Under the dome light in the van, discoloured by dust, his face was yellow. A sheen of sweat glistened on his forehead.

'There might be some doubt. It might belong to someone else.'

'What do you mean? All of it?'

'I've never known who owned the leasehold. That's held in some kind of trust and the solicitors do all the business. It's the freehold.'

'What are you talking about Tom?'

'When the Old Man died ... I found some papers in a foreign name. Tomas Dubrovic.' It was out. The name. He had resurrected it from the ash and suddenly the Old Man was there in the cramped space with them; the sardonic presence, mocking, making Tom's hands tremble slightly. He clasped them, knotting his fingers. This time he was going on with it. 'A seaman — a contract. This man ... signed on in Canada, on a ship called *Calypso* sailing to Adelaide.'

'What else?'

'Nothing much. A mining licence, a few letters.'

'Where are these things?'

'I burned them.'

'Why?' It was a whisper. 'Why now? He died *thirty years ago.*'

Tom flinched. 'Because I didn't want anyone to know ... There was only me. The Old Man died intestate.'

'But ... you would naturally inherit —'

'Zoe,' he whispered now, aware that he was loosening — preparing to remove — some central pin of his being: 'I may not be Thomas Drewe.'

Zoe was silent, staring at him. A sudden downpour pelted the aluminium roof. In the tightly closed van, the air was stuffy and damp. His legs were cramping and he rubbed them to relieve the muscles. He had yet to tell her ... other things. Perhaps he wouldn't tell her — yet.

'Who would you be, if you are not Thomas Drewe?'

'I don't know. I don't know who I am. I'm not sure about anything.' The rain had stopped as suddenly as it had begun. He stood up. 'I have to walk a bit, my legs. Too much driving.' He put on the jacket and hat he had hung on the peg inside the door and went out, closing the door behind him.

Zoe climbed out of the bunk and dressed. She rummaged in her paintbox and found the packet of thin cigars she occasionally smoked when painting. She put on warm socks and laced her boots firmly, twisting her hair up into a tight knot. She made herself another cup of coffee and sat on the step to wait for him. The acrid smoke from the cigar hung in front of her in the moisture-laden air. Kerb lights were scattered along the winding roadways, a dim glow through the dense shrubbery. The scattered vans were dark; couples, zipped up tight in their microcosms, maintaining their privacy. You got so good at it travelling around in a van, she thought. But why here? Why did he choose this dreary and banal place — from which there was no escape. The sea in front of them and the whole continent behind them. Trapped in their lives. That was a disadvantage of living on an island: wherever you went, sooner or later you came to the edge.

He appeared suddenly out of the dark, startling her. 'We'd better get some sleep,' he said. 'If the weather clears we'll get away early. We'll talk in the morning.'

In the limited space of the bunk they were separate. Silent.

Tom was aware that Zoe was deferring to him and he was grateful for it. The rain had gone, replaced by an icy wind off the Southern Ocean. They followed signs, through quiet neat streets, out into a countryside of green fenced fields. They stopped at a busy roadhouse on the outskirts for fuel. 'I think we should get some breakfast,' he said, 'it's going to be a long day.'

The acute drop in temperature was a shock after the months of travelling in the sun. They found a table and ordered substantial breakfasts. In the heated restaurant crowded with road train drivers making noisy conversation, they ventured cautiously.

'I brought the map in with me.' Zoe folded it and laid it on the table between them.

They studied it.

'We should make Ceduna tonight,' Tom said, 'Eucla tomorrow night, camp out the next night ... then Norseman.'

'Norseman?' Zoe was startled. 'I thought we'd be going south, to Esperance, home through Lake Grace.' The waitress arrived with steaming plates of eggs and bacon, and the map was hurriedly folded out of the way.

'Is it always this cold?' Tom asked the waitress.

'This is nothing,' she said, laughing. 'You're from the north? You can always tell.'

'We're heading west,' Tom said.

'Doing the round trip are you?'

He nodded.

With the heater on full blast they headed west along Eyre Highway, through fields green with winter pasture where sheep safely grazed. Surely *goodness and mercy* were part of it. A weak sun, in a pale rain-washed sky, cast a tepid warmth. Here and there along the highway, stands of huge gums shed a dappled light over the road, the cream and pink and white trunks a ripple of colour reeling past. It was Hans Heysen country; the placid colonial landscape. The neat villages, a cluster of buildings fringing the road, benign expressions of pastoral life. In the sweep and fold of the undulating country, wheat silos soared upwards, gleaming white.

Tom gestured: 'They paint the silos here. They don't bother in the west.'

'It's a part of the scene,' Zoe said. 'Neatness and order.' To her, the gleaming white granaries looked slightly sinister. They spoke of management and control, the land divided and fenced, pinned down tight at the corners by fenceposts; the abundance of alien grain husbanded and hoarded. 'They look like missile towers,' she said.

She folded the large touring map of Australia. The southern interior, from the Bight to the Northern Territory border, was blank. The small map of South Australia they had been using showed the Pitjantjatjara country, the restricted Woomera area, the railway line from Woomera to the restricted Maralinga Tjarutja land. There were tracks, dog fences; signs and symbols of access and prohibition. The large map showed only the boundary highways and the network of major internal roads.

'You could drive along this highway and have no idea that Maralinga is in there,' Zoe said. 'No signs, no indication of a nuclear landscape just over the hills.' She'd read about it: the tainted rain falling on the Aboriginal people who hadn't known what was happening; the aftermath ... the poisoned earth ... the survivors, wandering north and west, away from the inexplicable sickness that had fallen on their country. It was easier to delete it, leave it out; the map-makers deciding what the tourists needed to know. A quick safe passage around the edge was best for everyone. She put the map aside and searched for one of Western Australia.

'Why Norseman, Tom?' she said.

He had been waiting for her to ask.

He took his hand off the steering wheel and covered hers. Holding it tight. 'I'm going to go further up that way. To Cue, it's before Meekatharra.'

Zoe searched the fine red capillaries that covered the map of Western Australia, the small print that was a history of abandoned goldfields and visionary townsites.

'A miner's right was issued at Cue in 1894 in the name of Thomas Drewe. I have to start somewhere.'

'But there'll be nothing there now — '

'Zoe — I have to go.' How could he tell her: that he had to find a starting point. That, like the map, his interior was empty — a blank. That he could not bear the thought of going back and resuming a life that had, possibly, never belonged to him. He didn't want to set eyes on it, couldn't explain to her — or himself — that some kind of ... explosion within him had left him gutted. As long as he did not go back he could keep himself together. In a flash of insight he understood that his grandfather — the man — had done exactly that: kept things together, and fixed them in place by an act of will. A surge of energy, of adrenalin, made him lightheaded. A hundred years! He would end it, one way or another. He had to start again. It was the only way. He thought of the old peach tree near the river, gnarled and rotten. He had resisted rooting it out. It had been old when he first knew it. A graft from some unknown stock — gone wild and useless.

He had been carried there, lifted up, by the grandfather — the man. Thrust up into the blossom, sweet, the perfume of it, his hands clutching the soft petals, crushing them. The sound of bees loud in his ears, the sky above him, the warm sun. The man had lifted him high in his hands, offering him up, throwing him up and catching him, saying to him with each frightening upward thrust: This is paradise, this is paradise. He had clung to the man, dizzy, smelling the tobacco on the rough fabric of his jacket, burying his face in it.

His hands tightened on the wheel. He began to talk quietly to Zoe. There were many things to be attended to before they reached the border. She would have to be his agent in some of them.

Ceduna was an orderly town swept clean by the icy gales from the Southern Ocean. They parked on the beachfront amongst trees wind-formed into low shelters. In the morning, they walked into the shopping centre to buy groceries. Zoe hungered for fresh fruit and vegetables. Supplies, the attendant told her, would not arrive until Wednesday. She had forgotten — bemused by the neat houses and streets, the tidy footpaths. They were at the end of nowhere. There was no quick and easy access to anything. To live here required a clear head — a capacity to exist with minimal requirements; to adjust. They walked down to the shore, battling into the wind, hugging coats to their chests. Waves pounded the beach, sand whipped into their eyes. Turning their backs to the wind, they were pushed along the edge of the water, stumbling over piled seaweed.

Zoe opened cans and toasted stale bread for lunch. They drank tea and made tentative plans. During the night, the van creaked and swayed, the wind howling and hunting them in and out of their dreams.

At Eucla, they drove down to the coast, hurrying, bumping over the track. The remains of the telegraph outpost were buried in sand. A fragment of stone wall, a chimney, protruded from the fine white flow; the graceful arcs and rivulets temporarily held back by driftwood, or the whim of windflow. They were silent, looking at it. The final metaphor, Zoe thought: the land moving, shrouded in sea mist, ceaselessly laying bare or covering the past. Time was the illusion. They did not move through it, but within it. They lived on an island, captive and confined to what they had made of it.

They stopped in the afternoon for fuel and food. At Zoe's insistence, they had detoured from the highway to the cliffs. It was a delaying tactic. The road dissected flat barren country, a straight line ending at a barrier fence; beyond it was the ocean, a heaving glittering expanse. They walked along the pathway. The land ended in a sheer precipitous fall to the sea far below them. Zoe shielded her eyes, stumbling back to the truck. It had been there, waiting for her, this nightmare vision of the journey's end. She could not look at Tom walking there, pausing at the brink. The signs warned of sudden gusts of wind that made it dangerous to go too close, of crumbling limestone that could give way. One step too close and the body would fall, tumbling over and over, the scream uttered and gone in the instant of falling. She was close to tears. The country was so hard. It worked on you, stripping away. Leaving no safe place. Coming down on her, filling her mind, were the images: the Kathe Kollwitz faces again, black and white, distorted. She had asked for it, opened herself to it. Invited the awareness, the fragility of bone and muscle against such a landscape; the delicate flicker of life.

They camped in a stand of mallee, well back from the road. The litter scattered through the bush was evidence of countless other brief pauses crossing the Nullarbor.

The plain was not treeless, entirely. There were shallow gullies and undulations where mallee or saltbush grew, but it was vast; a transition that harrowed travellers with its flatness, its attenuated loss of perspective causing a kind of deprivation. Drivers were gripped with the fever to get through it, to reach the other side. Few, if any, lingered in this mono landscape. It had a reputation for inexplicable accidents: head-on collision, visitations and acts of unprovoked violence.

The light from their gas lamp threw a small circle and they were conscious of their isolation. In the shelter of a stand of mallee trees, they were protected from the wind which had harried them for days. They turned out the lamp and took folding chairs outside for the last time, the last night. The sky was clear of cloud and the stars blazed. In the crowded night sky they located their southern meridian, the axis from which they moved. The occasional roar of a road train rose and fell, disappearing quickly, east or west, leaving nothing to break the perfect closure of darkness.

'We've changed,' Zoe said. 'We've let go of so much. Life on the move is simple.'

'We left it too late,' Tom said.

'No. It's not too late. We have choices now.' Zoe was conscious of her own parallel journey, where it had taken her. 'The important thing is to judge ... how far to go. When to stop.'

'I have to do this myself,' Tom said. 'On my own. Keep it quiet.'

'I know.'

He told her that he knew the Old Man was Tomas. 'When I was a kid, he told me, one day, that he jumped ship when he reached Australia and went to the goldfields. It was just a yarn to me. I wasn't interested. He might have told me more ...'

'They're all gone now, with their secrets.' Zoe told him of her grandfather who had disappeared in the Murchison.

'They never found him?'

'Never a trace. Nothing.'

'Why didn't you tell me before?' The irony was apparent.

'It wasn't relevant ... before. It was a common story. The men went looking for gold — the women and children stayed behind. There was a photo of her, Ellen, and her sons, hanging in the hall. A lovely tall woman — with masses of dark hair and the saddest eyes.'

'Athol knew something,' Tom said. 'I know he did. He had something against me. What was so terrible in their lives that they never spoke of it? Left us nothing to go on. Knowing nothing, really, about who we are, where we come from.'

'Maybe it was the way they came here. So far. The way they survived was to block their memory. We can't imagine what it was like, living our entire lives in one small valley.'

'I don't need the rest of the world,' Tom said. 'The valley is my life. If it is not mine my life means nothing. I've wasted it. The Old Man was such a tough old bastard. What did he do to get it? That's what I'm afraid to find out.'

Zoe reached out and held his arm, smoothing the tense muscles. 'You could live without it, Tom.'

'I don't know if I can.'

'*They* had to, whoever was there before. They must have felt the same ...' (of course they had been there, in those fertile valleys, close to the coast).

'I can't feel that, Zoe. It's not real to me. I'm afraid of losing the lot.'

It was the closing of the circle, Zoe could see, an irony, keeping pace with them, slowly overtaking them. She saw the line of their journey on the map stretching out. The meandering line north, east, the downward pull to the south, the last turn west ... the distance travelled. This last interval, in a place defined by nullity: uninhabited, barren, a place of transition. 'We can't undo it,' she said. 'We have to keep going.'

It was not late. Darkness fell early and they'd had their evening meal before sunset, but it seemed to Zoe that they were enduring an endless night. She rose, chilled and cramped, and went inside, fumbling for matches to light the lamp, not caring who or what was attracted to the glow. She lit a gas ring to heat water and called to Tom. 'Come in. It's getting too cold. I'll make some toast.' She was aware of herself acting out women's habitual role: soothing, keeping normality alive with small ordinary acts, offering food and drink. She had to keep both of them going, get them back — out of this place. She was conscious of the man and woman they had been talking about, unknown figures, coming south, approaching a strange landfall; the awful inadvertence of history being set in motion.

A truck thundered past on the highway, sending a vibration through the earth. Momentarily Zoe felt herself to be at sea, the Southern Ocean rocking beneath her, and she remembered that under the Nullarbor there were caverns in the limestone reaching far inland, vast dark chambers remaining to be explored.

The Valley

They reached Norseman mid-afternoon. A town seemingly caught in a time-warp of the thirties or forties; hot and dry and without pretensions. The wide verandahs shading the shops had been there for a long time. Somewhere there would be a video shop and a lotto agency and whatever else the inhabitants needed for survival, but in the mid-afternoon the main street was deserted. In a creek bed, dusty white gums straggled, their leaves frayed and drooping. Tom and Zoe bought fuel and kept going.

It had been raining heavily. Pools of water were lying along road verges. Visible in patches of open country, everlastings stretched in every direction. Drifts of colour, pink and white and yellow. They drove through dense stands of vegetation, flowering shrubs; a vast wild garden scenting the air, inviting the traveller to stop and wander. It did not deceive Zoe. This was unfamiliar country, not quite desert, not anything they knew. On the map they were closer to home than they had been for months but it was as inaccessible as if they were in the centre.

It was not possible to go in a straight line. They must, first, go north to Coolgardie, then west through the wheatfields, then south to the last of the forest and the enfolding hills. Diverging, going around. Skirting impassable dunes, or the chains of salt lakes, or country so barren that roads had not been considered necessary. No one needed to go there, except the odd loner, the rabbit shooter, the dogger. On the map the lakes spread down from the north, the Great Sandy Desert fringing the Gibson Desert and fingering out into the Great Victoria Desert. One day the lakes could be sheeted with water, blue as the sky. Then almost overnight the water disappeared leaving a film of white, a salt crust over the soft mud. It was treacherous country for the inexperienced. If you were caught in the rain out there, travellers were told, stay where you are. Don't try and drive out. Most people never went near it. They clustered in the south-west corner, where it was safe.

He jumped ship in Esperance, Tom said. Probably walked up this way. It's how most of them got to the goldstrikes. By ship to Esperance and then ... the long walk.

The long walk. Drawn out. Everything was drawn out. It was the scale, the distance, the attenuation. A decision to change direction taken one day could be followed by days or weeks of travelling on a single road — the only road, with no sidetracks or detours possible. One had to live with one's decisions, Zoe thought. It made a difference. Nothing was straightforward or easy. On a map scattered with the blue of lakes there was no warning legend that dying of thirst and heat was a reality. The red line of roads stopped suddenly and beyond there was nothing. No way through. A season like this, with late heavy rains, washed out roads and cut communications. It isolated people. In a dry year, the wind blew away the feed and then the soil, and the people slowly withered, hanging on, hoping the drought would break, watching their stock die.

'I could never live here,' Zoe said.

'It's marginal country. People take the risk.'

'But would they dare to love it?' Zoe asked. 'They could never be sure of surviving. No matter how careful they were.' (It would dry you up, she thought. Make you hard. Life would be fine drawn, a thin thread of existence stretched to breaking point.) 'You better phone Jeremy tonight,' she reminded Tom. 'He'll be waiting to hear from you.'

'There's not much to say. I've arranged most of it. Jeremy knows all he needs to know for the time being. I'll sign power of attorney papers at the bank tomorrow and you can take them back with you.'

'Is all that necessary? How long are you going to be away?'

'I don't know. Something might come up. I might be hard to contact.'

Zoe was silent. Shrubbery was closing in on the narrow road. Long feathery fronds whipped against the sides of the vehicle. Occasional shallow sheets of water slowed them and the afternoon was slipping into dusk. They had passed no other vehicle for hours. Zoe closed her eyes to shut out the desolation, telling herself that she must not panic. She thought of the woman — her grandmother — when her husband went away the first time, and left her in a strange country. How had *she felt*? How had she managed? In the photograph she had been standing behind her two sons, staring at the photographer, serious, even remote — except for the eyes. The eyes gazed at the world with sadness. Even

195

as a child, Zoe had been made uneasy by the photograph hanging in the hall. She would avert her eyes from it. Her world was happy and secure. She didn't want to know anything different.

Ellen Madden was waiting. She had waited one whole year. Through the seasons changing. And now it was winter again and the hills were green. He was not coming back.
   He was gone.
Somewhere.
After the gold.

> *Mo ghra thu agus mo run*
> *Ni scaifidh ar mo chumha*
> *ata i lar mo chroi a bhru*
> *dunta suas go dluth*
> *mar a bheadh glas a bheadh ar thrunc*
> *'s go raghadh an cochair amu*

> *My love and my beloved*
> *my grief will not disperse*
> *but cram my heart's core.*
> *Shut firmly in*
> *like a trunk locked up*
> *when the key is lost.*

The utterance of the lament was fitting, the keening gave her grief dignity; but it was the syllables of her mother-tongue — the feel of it in her mouth — that soothed her. She was not much different from the old black woman who sat in the yard. Day after day. Watching her. The eyes sharp. They were both in extremis. When the old woman spoke to her, calling her in an unknown language, she would go to the door and answer her in Irish. Much passed between them, in time. Left alone, they were steadfast to each other.

Zoe wanted to talk to her sister Sophie. She needed Sophie.

'He *must* have come this way,' Tom said.

It had been easy. Tomas Dubrovic had slipped off the ship at Esperance in the melee of disembarking passengers. Families unloading their belongings and goldseekers pushing and shoving to find their gear in the pile of luggage heaped on the wharf. He had joined a family after a few days out from the port. No one asked questions. They fed him in return for a hand with their over-loaded dray. It was a wet season; the track was a quagmire and he strained alongside the man pushing the dray through the mud. There were flowers all the way. Children walked alongside picking them. Women smiled and the men were jovial, fresh and well set up at the start; a long caravan of innocents walking to the Promised Land. Before the year was out, half of them would be penniless and broken, or dead. He had driven the dray across the flowers (leaving a broken path behind him) to avoid the deep bog of the wheel ruts formed by those who were up ahead.

Tom had shut out what he didn't want to think about. He was surprised now at how easy it had been. They would be all right: Zoe, Jeremy, the orchard. Charley Byrne knew what had to be done as well as he did. He'd told Jeremy to give Charley a job for three months. He had no idea if he would be away that long, but he wanted time, plenty of time. They wouldn't miss him after a week or two. He didn't care anyway — that was the amazing thing. He didn't care. He was impatient to get out there. He would find something, or — he might find nothing. It didn't matter. He would find a place to start. He wondered, briefly, if he had gone mad. 'Lost it'. It was an old story. Everyone had a version: gone bush, took off, shot through. Maybe that's what her grandfather had done. All my life, Tom thought, I've done what was expected of me. He had struggled, at times, to keep it all together. He had learned well from the Old Man: you don't let go. You hold on to what's yours. Looking back, it seemed that everyone had wanted something from him. It was on the plateau, at Kings Canyon, that he had caught a glimpse of what he had lived with all his life, the bitter anger and the hurt behind the silence. He had the sense of a conspiracy to which everyone was privy, except him. He was on the outer. He felt a fool. The minute he had brought it into the open, his life had lost substance. He was a man of sixty-two years who did not know if he could keep hold of his land. He didn't even know who he was.

He could find little feeling in him for his family. They had led a charmed life, never had to battle for anything. None of them. He knew Zoe didn't understand why he was going. If he felt anything, it was a kind of resentment towards her — an envy of her ability to feel so intensely; that thing in her that was alive and strong and which, at times, he had tried to overpower. They all had it, the Maddens: that thing that he had wanted and felt deprived of and, at the same time, had been afraid to explore; a kind of certainty amongst themselves, a passionate resistance to accepting the way things were. They could be dangerous, people like that. This thing with Zoe and the Aborigines; questioning everything. What good did it do? People didn't want to have it thrust in their faces all the time. In Alice Springs, she had made him angry. *Cut the skin of this country,* she had said, *and it bleeds racism and brutality.* On her high horse. Judging everybody. Are you including me in that? he had asked her. *We are all in it,* she'd said. *We're all part of it.*

He had listened to the Aboriginal radio station in the centre, the men and women talking about their problems, what needed to be done. They were sure of themselves. Some of the names were familiar: Pearson. Dodson. Men who knew what they were talking about. Yunupingu and another one, Kevin somebody. Singers. Their music had a beat and a rhythm that was stirring. It was a movement gathering strength. It made him uneasy. What would he do if someone put a claim on the valley? That was something to think about. He must remind Zoe to say nothing. Especially not to her sister Clare — her husband was a land broker who would sell his soul to get his hands on two thousand hectares of prime country. There would be a few things to do in Coolgardie before he took off: making sure about the mining lease — that was the most important. It could have been what brought the Old Man to the valley in the first place. There had been a bit of a goldstrike there. Even a goldmine in the early days. And the other rare minerals. Worth more than the land.

Tomas had heard the Irishman talking about the southwest: sweet country, plenty of water, good soil, grow anything. His old woman was buying it up and he was going to retire there, be a gentleman farmer. The old diggers all had their dreams. They met each other again and again on the tracks, coming or going to another strike. He'd seen the Irishman at Munbinia, drunk on the Russian woman's shypoo. Down on his luck. Telling yarns for a feed and a drink: how Russian Jack had carried him on his barrow on the way to Halls Creek. Tomas had heard that story from half a dozen others. He had seen Russian Jack in Cue. Seven-foot tall and as wide across the shoulders as a bull, he was hard to miss. The Irishman had been heading up to Condon, on the coast near Derby. Hard country. The blacks were fierce in the ranges. South-west.

The train rocked him, chewing steadily into the distance. That's where he was going.

'I'm too tired for a caravan park tonight,' Zoe said as they entered the outskirts of Coolgardie. 'Let's find a motel.'

Tom agreed. It was the beginning. The move away from the close intimacy of the van into the wider space of a rented unit. They found a basic travellers' motel and, with the practice of months behind them, unpacked what they needed and carried it inside. Weariness made them slow. In the mundane room they saw themselves in the full-length mirror. They had come a long way and none of it showed. They looked middle-aged and tired. Nothing more. With a shower and a change of clothes they would fit in, as if they had never been away.

'I'm going to the shop,' she mouthed at Tom, while he was on the phone to Jeremy.

'Soph? It's Zoe.' She waited impatiently for the operator to connect the call — *will you acccept the charges?* —

'Who is it?' She heard Sophie's voice. 'From where?'

'Sophie,' Zoe said. 'Sophie, it's me. Zoe.'

'What are you doing in Coolgardie?' Sophie said. 'I was dreaming about you. Have you had an accident? Is Tom all right?'

'He's all right. We're both all right, but —'

'What's wrong then — ?' Sophie was impatient.

'Sophie. Listen. I'll be home in a couple of days. Tom's not coming with me.'

'What's the matter?'

'Did I wake you up?'

'Yes, it's nearly ten o'clock. What time is it there?'

A rush of affection swept Zoe. 'It's the same time here,

Sophie. We're only in Coolgardie. Tom is going up north, to the old goldfields. He wants to try and find out something about his grandfather. He's very upset.'

There was a silence on the line. 'Are you still there?' Zoe said. 'He's worried that he mightn't own the valley legally. Something to do with his grandfather's name. It has to be sorted out, the Old Man never left a will.'

'Does Jeremy know?'

'He knows there's a problem, but not what it is. Sophie, please don't talk to him about it, or anyone. Especially Clare. I just had to talk to you. Promise me you won't tell anybody.'

'I promise. What are *you* going to do?'

'I'll fly home.'

'Fly?'

'In an aeroplane. I haven't got wings.'

'You're no angel, I know that.'

They laughed noisily, a familiar release echoing down the line.

'Soph, I miss you.'

'You'll be all right. You're tough Zoe.'

'Am I? Soph, how much do you remember about our grandmother? You knew her better than I did.' Another silence. Zoe was getting prickles at the back of her neck.

'Quite a lot,' Sophie answered finally. 'I was nineteen when she died. She was in her nineties. Why do you want to know?'

'I've been thinking about her. It's strange but I feel her around me somehow. She keeps coming into my mind.'

'She was like that ...' Sophie was suddenly forceful. 'You come home Zoe. Let Tom go. He won't come to any harm.'

Zoe listened to her, knowing she was being persuaded, told what to do.

'Soph, you know something don't you? Tom said that Athol knew something.'

'I'll talk to you when you get home ... Oh, before I forget. Mim rang the other day.'

'Where is she?'

'In Tunisia, having a break. She was worried about you.'

She would be, Zoe thought. She would know *something* was going on. Time and distance didn't matter with some people.

'I have to go. Tom will be wondering where I am. Sorry I woke you.'

'It doesn't matter. I'm glad I know where you are.'

Tom was asleep when Zoe got back, weariness making charcoal shadows beneath his cheekbones and his eyes. She undressed quietly, climbing into the other side of the queen-size bed without disturbing him. He needed to sleep.

Drifting, Zoe could hear Sophie's voice. She could see her speaking, and behind her was the other face — shadowy — the *presence* of the other face. She could feel their concern and their interest — the women ... waiting for her. And somewhere at the back of them was Mim — anxious. The threads were tightening. Drawing her back.

The memory was vivid. The four of them: Dolly with her translucent skin and fiery hair, an aureole of light and fire, the halo of an early death already around her; Sophie and Clare, self-possessed and daring, and herself, much younger, edgy and nervous. They were down at the river where the boundary fences met, waiting for the rude silent boy. He would come. He always came — if they waited long enough.

He was there, standing on his side of the fence, looking at them.

'What do *you* want?' Sophie was daring him.

'You stay off our property,' he said.

'What are you scared of?' they taunted him.

'I'm not scared,' he said.

'Well, come over here then,' Clare had called out. 'Prove it.'

He had climbed through the fence and they had waited, tense and excited, letting him come closer, closer, until they could pelt him with the balls of mud they had ready. Screaming and laughing, pelting him with mud, and then running, scrambling up the hill, making the sheep run. He had been their plaything; to be taunted and drawn out and then cruelly demolished. He lived up there, on the other side of the river through the fence. He belonged to them, part of their secret exciting existence.

Zoe woke to the clatter of breakfast being slid through the hatch. Tom drew the curtains back. Outside a brassy sun shone on the ordinariness of their surroundings.

They drove the short distance into Kalgoorlie, the wide streets filled with traffic, the nineteenth-century hotels with their rococo balconies shading the sidewalks. A city poised over the hollow shafts of goldmines. On the outskirts, huge open-cut mines sliced into the earth. Every rock would be overturned, every grain sifted. The air was acrid, catching in the throat. The citizens breathed the air and coughed. It was part of the price.

Tom and Zoe went about their business with wooden bodies, exhausted by the unaccustomed noise and the sultry heat. They went to a travel agency and booked

Zoe's flight for early the next morning. In the bank Tom signed his name — Thomas Drewe — and passed it over to Zoe. She signed under Jeremy's signature. Tom bought boots and a broad-brimmed hat. In the motel, he tried the hat on, embarrassed when he caught Zoe watching him in the mirror.

In the airconditioned room, with the curtains drawn to shut out the harsh light, they separated their belongings. Zoe selected the books and photographs she wanted to take with her, piling the shabby shorts and shirts she'd worn day after day on top of them. There wasn't much she needed. Some of it she discarded. Underlying their calm, a tension pulled gently between them; the history of their lives together, keeping them in balance. She helped him rearrange his things in the space she had made in the campervan.

'Do you want this?' he asked. It was her old sewing tin — which she seemed to have had all her life. The red and gold pattern was scratched and worn, but the lid still fitted tight — she kept odds and ends in it. Things she didn't want to lose.

She thought about it. 'Leave it in the van, it would be awkward to carry. If you find any gold lying around you can put it in there.'

After eating a meal, they went for a walk to get out of the motel room. Somewhere a dog barked, a domestic sound. People were driving home from work in dust-stained vehicles. A flock of birds flew over, circling, then heading off. The heat was going quickly. In an hour or two it would be replaced by a sharp chill.

They mentioned things to each other as they thought of them. Practical things; the preparation.

In the pre-dawn they drove to the airport. Men with brief-cases and bags heavy with surveying instruments stood around outside, smoking last cigarettes. Inside, a few women nursing sleepy children waited. A family of Aborigines talked and laughed, children playing noisily.

'I'll telephone when I can,' Tom said. 'It shouldn't be a problem.'

He was ready to go, she saw. Poised and already distanced from her. Because she knew him so well she was aware of the eagerness he was keeping down. In turn she suppressed her anxiety at leave-taking.

'I'll be home tonight,' she said.

The boarding call came and they held each other. Tightly. Tom handed Zoe a plastic carry bag. 'It's your sewing tin,' he said. 'You might need it.'

'Don't hurry,' she told him. 'Be patient.'

It was the best she could do. It was his journey.

As the plane circled before settling to its course, she saw, in a brief sweep, the endless plain denuded of trees by countless goldminers. It stretched to the horizon, criss-crossed with lines: tracks leading nowhere. As the plane gained height, Zoe saw sheets of sparkling blue in the dawn sunlight; the watershed of unseasonal rains. She saw the patterns of the earth reduced to their essential geometry: the shadow and angle of a declivity, the exquisite shading of red to pink of bare ground pockmarked by mines. She craned to see as much as she could. The sensate body of the land displayed itself for her: the fluid play of undulating contours, the minimalist beauty of burnt country, a cicatrice pattern of ebony on red, breathtaking in its symmetry. It flexed and moved under the influence of sun and cloud, shapes forming and dissolving; a land mass alive and potent within itself. Very briefly she understood how an intimate and profound knowledge of the land could be encoded into an abstraction and remain locked in the mind; *the idea of it* absorbed forever. He was down there somewhere. A minute organism. Taken in by it. She felt, in a physical sense, the snapping of the connection between them; the unseeing, unfeeling hiatus of absence. He was lost in it.

Tomas Dubrovic watched, with the eyes of the world-weary, the unfolding countryside, the steep wooded hills and cleared pastures, the deep ravines through which the line cut its way, following the Avon River. The steam engine pulled its load of carriages and freight up the incline of the escarpment. Below, on the coastal plain, was the city; the Capital. A smudge of smoke and a distant cluster of buildings fringing a wide expanse of river — and, beyond that, the ocean. He liked the boldness of the city's extreme isolation, its fragile hold on the lip between land and sea; as insubstantial as a mirage. He would take his time. He was not in a hurry.

In the valley, Ellen Madden waited. It was not finished. She walked in the dark down to the slab fence and rough gate and stood there. Listening. She was not frightened alone with her sons in the dense dark forest which stretched up the slopes. She had wooed it in her own way and come to terms with it. She was waiting for the sound of someone coming. She pulled her shawl tighter around her shoulders against the damp mist curling out of the river, folding her arms across her breasts.

Someone would come.

Zoe had insisted that she wanted to make her own way home. All she wanted was for someone to take her car to the airport. Her excuse was that she did not know when she could get a flight on the small airline that serviced the rural city forty kilometres from the valley. She wanted the time, the brief period alone before her return. She had been lucky. It was only midday and already she was sitting behind the wheel of her old Mercedes; a countrywoman's car, safe and reliable on the narrow twisting country roads and a symbol of disregard for changing values. She had piled her luggage in the boot and was ready to go.

Zoe drove slowly out of the car park, waiting to merge into the highway traffic, undecided whether she would drive into town and see Jeremy, or go home. She was not looking forward to meeting her son, unsure of what she would tell him. At the roundabout she slowed and turned, taking the road out of town. She knew every bend and hollow in the road. Every farm and shed, and many of the people along the way. As she left the traffic behind and gathered speed she felt relieved. She had breathing space. For a couple of hours she was on her own.

As the country began to rise gently towards the steep scarp, Zoe started to feel apprehensive. There was anxiety, almost a sense of panic, at re-entering the landscape of enclosing hills and forest, the last stands of jarrah. She had adjusted to the dimension of limitless space and light, beneath a vertiginous blue dome.

The road fell in a sharp decline, shadowed by trees at its base. A curving bend and the first of the many narrow bridges over the winding river checked her speed. She felt unsure of her judgement. It was months since she had driven a car. The road wound and turned, the slopes pressing in close on each side. The cleared hillsides were a welcome break from the shadow of the timbered gullies.

On the short flight from Perth she had been absorbed in the undulation of the escarpment which followed the coast south. The coastal plain was narrow, bordered by the line of sand dunes and ocean to the west and then the hills, folded and pleated in on themselves, within which the life was hidden, turned inward and concealed. There was no sign of the small hamlets she knew were there. The only signs of life were the ploughed paddocks, the chocolate squares of tilled earth. The merest edge, confined by ocean and escarpment. She felt a wrench of loss for the vast freeing openness she had left behind.

Approaching the farm, she didn't know how to think of it. She had no vision of it in her mind, no sense of the shape or contour. It was the road home. On impulse, she passed by the white gateposts which marked the entry to the orchard.

The gravel driveway to the old stone house, two kilometres further on, was worn through and potholed in places. The garden was overgrown, a wilderness of shrubs unpruned and grown into each other. The jonquils were still out, she noticed, and the hyacinths. Succulent spring grass grew thick up to the edge of the slate verandah. Zoe stopped the car and walked on the gravel path around to the side door. The rose trellis was sagging. She walked into the hall, past the coat rack with its collection of odd hats and jackets, smelling the familiar smells: dust, dried roses, lemons, woodsmoke; it never seemed to change. She stood in the kitchen doorway looking at Sophie asleep in her chair near the Aga range. Like the house, Sophie was old, subsiding softly into her bones. The room was warm and cluttered and shabby. On the wall hung the overlarge, roughly carved crucifix. On hooks, hanging from the shelf above the range, were bunches of onions and drying herbs from the garden. Old newspapers were piled in a corner. Zoe loved it passionately.

'Sophie,' she said quietly. 'I'm home.' Her sister woke with a start.

Zoe bent down and kissed her.

'You gave me a fright,' she said, 'I was just having forty winks. When did you get here?'

'Just now.' Zoe moved the kettle onto the stove. 'Tea or coffee?'

'Tea.'

They sat by the fire, from habit, sipping their tea, exchanging news. Laughing themselves to tears over Sophie's account of the 'Great Mushroom Scare'. Suddenly chastened as Sophie told Zoe of the fights in the pub on Friday night between the timbermill workers and the conservationists who had come to town to try and stop clearfelling the old forest. 'The town is dying,' Sophie said. 'The young ones go to the city and their fathers live in the past.'

Zoe had noticed something hanging in the window, a string of objects knotted into a pendant. She got up to look at it. Pebbles and brilliant green and red parrot feathers. 'Sophie, you've been having visitors.'

'Oh, they don't hurt anyone. They're interesting. They call themselves ferals,' she said and laughed. 'They play the same games we used to ... remember the cave? They're about as feral as my chickens. I cook them a stew now and again. It's been a cold winter.'

Zoe sat down, slumping in the old chair with its nest of lumpy cushions. 'Tell me what you know, Sophie, before I go up the hill.' (It was the old way of putting it, their private way of designating the Drewe property and the house that she'd taken over.)

Sophie was reluctant, slow to speak. Zoe felt again the tremor of panic at what she might hear. 'It was old Ellen,' Sophie said finally. 'She made an arrangement with Tom's grandfather. She knew he wasn't an Englishman.'

Zoe was still. 'Did she know who he was?'

'I don't know,' Sophie said. 'It suited Ellen.'

'What kind of arrangement?'

'Well, she couldn't do anything with the land after Dennis disappeared.'

'*She owned it?*'

Sophie nodded. 'The whole valley. She was just hanging on. She wouldn't sell to the English. And most of them — all of them around here with money — were English, if you think about it.'

'How did you find out?'

'She told me some of it; I used to look after her when she was old, and Athol — told me some of it.'

'So this man, calling himself Thomas Drewe, bought it?'

Sophie was fussing with the tea, getting up to rummage for a biscuit. 'Not all of it.'

'What do you mean?'

'She sold him half of it.'

'*Half ...*' Zoe forced herself to be calm. 'Who did she sell the other half to?'

'She didn't sell it.' Sophie sat down again with a thud. 'I've been dreading this. I hoped I'd die in my sleep and not have to deal with it. I own it,' she said. They stared at each other.

It had been a very long day. Just that morning she had let go of Tom (and she had yet to go home and see Jeremy and Liz and her grandchildren). Two weeks ago she had been in the centre. Already it seemed an irretrievable dream.

'Walk down to the river with me,' she said to Sophie. She waited at the door while Sophie changed her shoes.

'It's pretty wet,' Sophie said.

They walked down the pathway of pine needles through the thick growth of bracken to the high earth bank of the river. The deep narrow channel was flowing swiftly, the water stained brown by tannin from bark and leaves.

'I had the feeling I didn't want to come home,' Zoe said. 'I wasn't ready.' She sat on a fallen log watching the water. She sighed. 'How did you end up with it, Soph?'

'It's a long story.' Sophie was big and solid standing there, her old shoes sinking into the wet earth. 'I always wanted it,' she said. 'Ellen knew that. Old Drewe kept at her, but she wouldn't part with it. Men don't always settle, she used to say to me. They go away. And when you need them they are not there. She left it to me because I was young and I promised her I would look after it.'

Zoe shivered in the shade of the trees. 'Do you know what her life was like in Ireland?'

'She never spoke of it. Except, she told me once, she left in anger. I think she grieved all her life.'

On the deck of Patrick Lynch's boat I sat in woeful plight.
Through my sighing all the weary day, and weeping all
the night;

Sophie quoted softly, a slight assumed lilt in her voice.

And I sailing, sailing swiftly from the county of Mayo.

'I remember,' Zoe said. 'Her eyes, in the photograph, they haunted me as a child. They haunt me still I suppose. And it's not finished yet, is it?'

'No. You will have to think what to do next, Zoe. I've left it to you.'

The weight of Sophie's words settled on Zoe. Through the

211

shadow of the trees on the bank of the river she could see the green hillside, bright in the sunshine; open to the light.

They walked arm in arm back to the house set against the slope on the high bank of the river. The local stone from which it was built glowed soft pink and russet in the late afternoon sun. 'I love it,' Sophie said quietly. 'It's been enough.'

'What about Athol?' Zoe asked.

'Athol — he was bitter,' Sophie said. 'It should have all been his, he thought. Her only son — after Dan died. And then — she passed him over — for me.'

Aftershocks ... 'It must have been a relief when I came back from university and married Tom,' Zoe said.

'It's strange how things work out,' Sophie said softly.

A wave of exhaustion hit Zoe. All the pieces of her life were in realignment. 'I'll have to go, they'll be wondering what's happened to me. I'll come back tonight.'

Zoe drove slowly up through the orchard, the ranks of trees loaded with ripening fruit, the diagonal striations of the raspberry canes stitched into the lower slopes. Looking with the eye of a stranger, seeking the underlying sense of the land, trying to gauge what she was feeling. Its soft fertility caused a quiver in her flesh, a tightening of her skin; use had made it vulnerable. The house was stark white against the exposed granite, and behind it, somewhere, was the nameless grave of the unloved son. Tom's father. She would have to do something about that.

She reached for Tom, the sense of him. Angry for him, the use that had been made of him; the purpose they had both served. *Come back*, she willed him. *Come back. Here is where you should be.* She saw Sophie and herself, drawn unwittingly into the long playing out of an old grief and understood, for herself, the melancholy of separation.

Her son was waiting for her on the steps, self-possessed and unaware. 'I was beginning to worry about you,' he said. 'And Dad?' he asked as they went inside. 'How is he? Where is he now?'

Zoe was firm. 'He'll be in touch,' she said. 'There's no hurry.'

'I need to know —'

She smiled. 'Give him time. We'll wait.'

After dinner, Zoe made her excuses. She would stay with Sophie for a couple of days. Jeremy and Liz were having weekend guests — it was easier — she was too tired to be sociable. She collected overnight things and promised to come up early in the morning. Jeremy was difficult about letting her walk down alone.

'Is there anything different that I should be concerned about?' she asked.

'No. Nothing's changed.'

'I'll take a torch.' She left them by the fire, sipping their port, wondering what to make of her.

Zoe felt drained. She walked slowly, swinging the torch, watching her feet on the earthen path where it cut across the slope of the hill. Down the bottom she could see the glow of light from Sophie's place. Halfway down she stopped and sat on a familiar rock. She put out the torch to save the batteries and huddled her coat around her. It was cold. The damp air, as she breathed it in, smelled of leaf mould. Above her, light cloud drifted across the moon. There were few stars. In the dark, she waited for a sense of the land's contours to come to her. She felt the deep precipitous fall of the eroded scarp. She was aware of the granite mass beneath the soil. She knew that in the morning the river would be hidden in mist, and, in the sunlight, yellow soursob and pinks would be a drift of colour beneath the fruit trees. Somewhere high up, on the treeline, something screamed — a fox hunting; an alien unwanted marauder. She thought of the slow backward drift that had taken hold of her and Tom as they travelled, moving them toward their beginning; the ancestral journeys from one place to another. Refugees — or fugitives — with no way back. Tenacious and unwilling to let go. It was like a blind faith: the colonial myth that the New World supplanted the old. It didn't work like that.

She waited, as she had in other places, for something to happen: an idea, a sense, an image that would let her know if she was home. Like her, the earth around her was tired. The soil had been stripped and worked hard for nearly a hundred years. How much more would it bear? She heard, above her head, the swish of wings: an owl, intent on its prey. Quietly, deeply hidden, life went on. The old woman had been shrewd to defer the handover of the land. And to channel it through Sophie. *Let time pass. Don't yield.* Ellen could have said that — or thought it. But Zoe was different. She knew too much. She could no longer engage with the shifting patterns of the surface, but she feared the dark, unchanging sub-strata. It could claim her, like it had Sophie. She hunched her shoulders against the trouble ahead. From somewhere a drift of air played over her face, carrying a fragrance; a sweet familiar breath. Boronia. A late season. She got up and continued down the path, talking to the old woman; the restless spirit. *It's enough,* she said. *Old Woman. No more grief. That's finished now. And all you others, from the beginning,* she said, cautious in acknowledging their loss. *Please rest.* She walked quickly, sure-footed on the path.

In the open doorway Sophie waited for her. 'I'd just about given you up,' she said. They sat by the kitchen range sipping a nightcap of the good whiskey, while the sheets for Zoe's bed warmed up.

Zoe slept late and woke to find Sophie offering her tea and toast on the old veined china.

'This room is musty,' Sophie said, and went to open the French doors. Light streamed in, the cold morning air carrying the scent of damp earth, the cloying sweetness of jonquils.

In a corner stood the old upright piano. This had been their mother's music room.

'Do you ever play?' Zoe asked.

'The felts are gone.' Sophie lifted the lid and struck a note. It echoed, strident and off key, releasing a faint odour into the room. Zoe breathed it in: beeswax, camphor, ivory; the smell of past music.

The telephone rang in the kitchen and Sophie hurried to answer it, Zoe following her, the polished boards cold under her bare feet.

'Is it ... ?'

'It's Tom,' Sophie mouthed, as she handed her the phone.

'Where are you?' The first question always asked of a missing person.

She strained to hear him over a bad line. Making up her mind ... Sophie was looking at her ... waiting. 'Tom — can you hear me? Tom, are you there?' His voice had broken up, distorted by distance. Zoe put the receiver down. 'He's gone,' she said. 'It's raining up there. He's stranded on a station somewhere.'

She walked over to the open kitchen window, leaning on the sill. She could hear the river. It was always there, indistinct at first, but it became clearer when you listened. 'I'll tell him later. When he comes back.'

'There's plenty of time,' Sophie said, filling the space beside her. 'Plenty of time.'